Inked Nights

Also from Carrie Ann Ryan

Montgomery Ink
Book 0.5: *Ink Inspired*
Book 0.6: *Ink Reunited*
Book 1: *Delicate Ink*
Book 1.5: *Forever Ink*
Book 2: *Tempting Boundaries*
Book 4: *Harder than Words*
Book 4: *Written in Ink*
Book 4.5: *Hidden Ink*
Book 5: *Ink Enduring*
Book 6: *Ink Exposed*
Book 6.5: *Adoring Ink*
Book 6.6 *Love, Honor, and Ink*
Book 7: *Inked Expressions*
Book 7.3: *Dropout*
Book 7.5: *Executive Ink*
Book 8*: Inked Memories*
Book 8.5: *Inked Nights*
Book 8.7: *Second Chance Ink*

Montgomery Ink: Colorado Springs
Book 1: *Fallen Ink*
Book 2: *Restless Ink*
Book 3: *Jagged Ink*

The Gallagher Brothers Series:
A Montgomery Ink Spin Off Series
Book 1: *Love Restored*
Book 2: *Passion Restored*
Book 3: *Hope Restored*

The Whiskey and Lies Series:
A Montgomery Ink Spin Off Series
Book 1: *Whiskey Secrets*
Book 2: *Whiskey Reveals*
Book 3: *Whiskey Undone*

Inked Nights
A Montgomery Ink Novella

By Carrie Ann Ryan

1001 Dark Nights

EVIL EYE
CONCEPTS

Inked Nights
A Montgomery Ink Novella
By Carrie Ann Ryan

1001 Dark Nights

Copyright 2018 Carrie Ann Ryan
ISBN: 978-1-945920-97-4

Foreword: Copyright 2014 M. J. Rose

Published by Evil Eye Concepts, Incorporated

Acknowledgments from the Author

This book was far different than what I'd thought it would be. When I first met Derek back in 2014 in the first of the Montgomery Ink series, I thought I knew his past. It turns out, my own life found itself mirroring that story far too much and I changed what Derek had once been into who he needed to be for myself and for him.

This wasn't the story I thought I would write and yet it was the story I needed to write. And I want to thank Chelle, Liz, and Jillian for talking it over with me, and MJ and Liz for creating such an amazing series that I'm blessed to be part of.

Thank you.

Sign up for the 1001 Dark Nights Newsletter
and be entered to win a Tiffany Key necklace.

There's a contest every month!

Go to www.1001DarkNights.com to subscribe.

As a bonus, all subscribers will receive a free copy of
Discovery Bundle Three
Featuring stories by
Sidney Bristol, Darcy Burke, T. Gephart
Stacey Kennedy, Adriana Locke
JB Salsbury, and Erika Wilde

One Thousand and One Dark Nights

Once upon a time, in the future...

*I was a student fascinated with stories and learning.
I studied philosophy, poetry, history, the occult, and
the art and science of love and magic. I had a vast
library at my father's home and collected thousands
of volumes of fantastic tales.*

*I learned all about ancient races and bygone
times. About myths and legends and dreams of all
people through the millennium. And the more I read
the stronger my imagination grew until I discovered
that I was able to travel into the stories... to actually
become part of them.*

*I wish I could say that I listened to my teacher
and respected my gift, as I ought to have. If I had, I
would not be telling you this tale now.
But I was foolhardy and confused, showing off
with bravery.*

*One afternoon, curious about the myth of the
Arabian Nights, I traveled back to ancient Persia to
see for myself if it was true that every day Shahryar
(Persian: شهريار, "king") married a new virgin, and then
sent yesterday's wife to be beheaded. It was written
and I had read, that by the time he met Scheherazade,
the vizier's daughter, he'd killed one thousand
women.*

*Something went wrong with my efforts. I arrived
in the midst of the story and somehow exchanged
places with Scheherazade – a phenomena that had
never occurred before and that still to this day, I
cannot explain.*

*Now I am trapped in that ancient past. I have
taken on Scheherazade's life and the only way I can
protect myself and stay alive is to do what she did to
protect herself and stay alive.*

*Every night the King calls for me and listens as I spin tales.
And when the evening ends and dawn breaks, I stop at a
point that leaves him breathless and yearning for more.
And so the King spares my life for one more day, so that
he might hear the rest of my dark tale.*

*As soon as I finish a story... I begin a new
one... like the one that you, dear reader, have before
you now.*

Chapter One

Pebbled flesh.

Quick intakes of breath.

Long sighs turning to moans.

That's what awaited Olivia Madison, and she knew it. She'd always known it. She'd rake her fingernails down his back, arch into him, and let herself be taken in the most primal way. And then she'd walk away again without looking back. They'd have a drink. They'd fuck. They'd keep it to only those details. There would be no last names, no promises. Exactly how they wanted it. And in a month, they'd do it again.

It was her thrill, her deepest secret.

Well, not her *deepest*, but the only one she could face.

Just one more time. That's what Olivia had told herself last month, and yet, she knew she would be back for more. She'd always be back for more when it came to him.

Because that was how it was, and she wasn't sure it would ever change. She wasn't sure she needed it to change. Wasn't sure she *wanted* it to change.

But she was going to push those thoughts from her mind. Because tonight was about one thing. Hot, unadulterated sex. At least that's what she kept telling herself. Because there was no way that Olivia was going to fall for the man she didn't know. She might know his body just as much as he knew hers, but that was it.

She didn't even know what his favorite drink was. She swore he ordered a different one each time they were out together just to throw her off. She'd found herself doing the same, but maybe not for the same reasons. She just liked variety, liked knowing that she didn't have to commit to something as simple as a drink.

The only commitment she allowed herself was one night a month with a man named *D*. He knew her as *O*.

And every time he called her that, there was a little laughter in his eyes because he had indeed given her a few *O*s along the way.

She mentally rolled her eyes at the horrendous joke and took a sip of her lemon drop martini. Tonight, she'd wanted something extra sweet to get the bitter taste of regret out of her mouth. For some reason, this night felt different than previous months. Maybe she was just getting old, or the fragile relationship she had with her stranger was getting stale, but either way, she felt like this might be the last one. And maybe it needed to be.

Having sex with a stranger with no promises and no strings once a month for as long as it had been going on seemed crazy and a little as if she were playing with fire. She often wondered what the manager or bartender at this hotel thought of them. Because this wasn't the first time she'd seen the same guy behind the bar, wasn't even the first time she'd seen the concierge.

Olivia wasn't the one who booked the hotel room; that had always been the job of the other person in this strange relationship.

She just had to show up at the same time every month, sip her drink, and wait. And the thrill of that set her on edge. She knew it was wrong, knew she was consistently making the same mistakes, but she didn't care, not when it came to him. And perhaps that was the greatest mistake of all.

"I see we meet again."

That deep voice went straight to her lady parts, sending shivers down her spine and making her want to arch her back like a cat. She loved that voice, loved that growl. She especially loved it when he was groaning above her as he made both of them slide into sweet ecstasy.

She looked over her shoulder and raised a brow, doing her best to look as sultry as possible. She knew she was sexy, knew she had all the right curves. She'd even learned how to dress those curves and apply just the right amount of makeup to enhance the smokiness of her eyes, the plumpness of her lips, and the angles of her cheekbones.

She knew all of that, and had looked up tutorials and gone shopping with her friends to ensure that she knew the rules of this particular game she played.

As soon as she caught the look in D's eyes, she knew she had played things just right—at least for tonight.

She had chosen a champagne-colored cold-shoulder dress. There was a split in the side of the skirt that showed just the barest bit of thigh that she knew he'd already noticed, twice. She'd put her long, wavy hair up in a sort of twist along the back of her head, only because she loved the way he pulled out the pins and let her hair tumble down her back.

Yes, she dressed for him, and she probably shouldn't have. But she did.

"You say that as if you're surprised." She smiled, not able to help herself. She wasn't some femme fatale that could act all unaffected, even if she tried. But she liked this man, even if she didn't know exactly who he was. She liked their game, liked what they had, even if it was just an illusion. She would have tonight, and in the morning, she would wonder why she allowed herself to remain in this situation, but then she would forget again and only remember him.

D gave her a long look before taking the seat next to her at the bar. "I always am. Just as you always seem surprised to see me walking toward you. If only for a moment."

"I like how you act as if you know me."

He leaned down closer to her face, his warm breath on her neck. "Sugar, I know you."

That made her snort. She couldn't help it. Hence why she wasn't that femme fatale she tried to dress as.

"Are you laughing at me?" he asked, a clearly fake put-upon look on his face. "You saying I don't know you?"

She shook her head as the bartender came over to take D's drink order. Johnny Walker Black this time. Interesting. Talk about smooth and smoky.

"No, I wasn't laughing at that, but isn't the whole point of...*this*, that we don't know each other?" She held out her hand when he would have answered. She didn't need to know what he had to say about their arrangement. It was weird enough already, even with how hot it was. "I was snorting at the whole 'sugar' thing. I've never heard you call me that, and we live in Denver, not the south. I don't know where you picked that up."

D shrugged, taking a sip of his drink. "A client said it. I must have subconsciously absorbed it."

It was on her tongue to ask him what kind of client, but that wasn't who she and D were to each other. She would do well to remember that. Even D seemed a little annoyed that he'd let that bit of his life slip. But instead of saying more, he took another sip of his scotch, then turned on the stool so his legs were caging hers. She didn't mind. At this point, she'd use any excuse to get closer to him, to have him touch her, even if it broke her in the end.

Yes, she was an idiot, but she couldn't help it.

Not with D.

Because she knew his rules, too.

One night a month.

No last names…or firsts for that matter.

No promises.

She let out a deep breath, aware that he was watching her. She needed to stop thinking about what she shouldn't want and just live in the moment. It was how she'd gone through every other month in the past with D, and it would be how she got through tonight, too.

"I'm glad you made it," she said, honestly. Probably too honestly, but she was doing her best not to question herself the entire night like she was prone to do. The only time she was able to forget everything was when D helped her, and she knew she couldn't always rely on that.

He studied her face, and she wondered what he saw. Wondered why she cared.

"I'm glad I did, too." He held up his glass, and she did the same, knowing their routine was anything but. "To inked nights."

She grinned. "Always."

She knew the ink that was hidden under his clothes just as he knew the ink that lay under hers. Inked nights had been a passing comment between the two of them on their first night and had been their toast ever since.

Olivia took a sip of her drink, the sweetness coating her tongue. When he reached out and wiped some of the sugar from her lip, she flicked out her tongue, needing to taste him, as well.

"Sugar," he said with a wink, and she couldn't help but smile. "Indeed."

They finished their drinks, looking at only each other. For all she knew, there could be hundreds of people around them, and yet he was it for her. And maybe, just maybe, she was it for him. She'd already paid for her martini since she didn't have a room, and D set out cash next to his drink, not bothering to wait for a bill. They never paid for each other's drinks, never got close enough to a receipt to see a name. And while he paid for the hotel room, they didn't bother with gifts or fancy words either.

Their nights were just about the two of them.

When he slid off his stool and took her hand, she knew she would follow, knew she would soon be in a bed they shared but didn't own. Others might look at them, wonder, or *know*, but nobody but D mattered in her mind—at least for this moment. They went into the elevator together but weren't alone. There would be no teases, no touches as they waited to arrive on their floor. Of course, there never were because it was only them when they were within the walls of the hotel room. He never touched her beyond taking her hand or guiding her with his hand on the small of her back.

His presence was foreplay enough for her. There didn't need to be extra touches or caresses. As soon as the hotel room door closed behind them, however, everything would change.

Just like she wanted, just like she *needed* it to.

D pressed the key against the sensor, and as soon as the green light lit, she knew this was it. Just the two of them and no one else. When the door closed behind them, her pulse pounded, and she swallowed hard, knowing that it was *time*.

Finally.

"I'm going to unzip that dress, but not before I have those panties of yours. Take them off."

She loved the way his voice sent shivers down her body. "I'm not wearing any."

He let out a rough curse and then was on her, his mouth on hers, his hands running down her sides. When she arched against him, her back against the door, and her breath coming in pants, he pulled away, his gaze roaming over her body.

"No panties? You were down in that lobby, with all those other men around, without wearing panties?"

She licked her lips, needing more. Needing him. "I figured it would save time."

In answer, his eyes got impossibly darker, and his hand snaked between her legs. When he found her hot flesh, his fingers delving between her soaking folds, her eyes rolled back, and she rotated her hips.

"Eyes on me, O. Let me see those eyes when I make you come on my hand. I want you drenched. So wet that I'm going to take my time licking every drop. Now look at me, O. Feel my fingers inside you. Feel me tease then thrust. Then come, right here. Right now. Can you do that, O? Can you come for me?"

She could have said "yes" right then. Could have come on his hand and finished their first round. But she wanted it to last.

She needed it to last.

"Make it worth it."

He grinned then, his eyes dancing. Then he *moved*. His fingers curled, touching her in just the right spot so she came without knowing she was even that close. She'd thought she could make it last.

But she never could when it came to D and his talented fingers.

And his talented tongue.

Or his talented dick.

"That's it. I knew you'd be fucking beautiful. You always are."

Then, he unzipped her dress, and she stepped out of it and her shoes. He undid the pins in her hair, letting the mass tumble down her back. It was just as sensual as she'd thought it would be, made her just as needy.

She could fall in love with this man. This stranger who wasn't a stranger.

She quickly pushed that thought out of her mind and came back to the present, to the moment that was just O and D.

"I can't believe you weren't wearing panties," he whispered against her lips, undoing her bra. It fell to the floor, and soon she was naked while he was fully dressed, and she couldn't help but wonder why that turned her on so much.

"You're still wearing your clothes." A kiss. A touch. A lick. A graze against her nipple. He knew what he was doing. Knew her body better than anyone but her. It should have worried her, and it probably would later. But for now, it was all about him.

And her.

"I can fix that."

He stripped as he led her to the bed, their bodies sliding against one another. Then he was naked and rolling on a condom. He was so quick that she almost missed a glance at his cock since she loved looking at his length, his girth, every inch of him. But she would later, she promised herself that much.

"On your back, O. Let me take care of you."

"As long as I can take care of you, too."

"Wouldn't dream of having it any other way," he said with a wink.

She let out a breath, trying to act calmer than she actually was. When he slid into her, inch by slow inch, she gasped, needing more of him. Her legs wrapped around his waist and her fingers dug into his back. He stretched her, moved within her, and made her eyes roll back once again.

He thrust in and out, his face buried against her neck as they slowly made love. She couldn't think of it any other way, not when they were so in tune with one another. She'd call it screwing or fucking or something else later, but not right then.

"D," she whispered, and he moved faster. Harder. And she met him thrust for thrust, ache for ache.

"Call me Derek, when you scream out my name, call me Derek." Then he slammed into her, and she came, screaming his name, a name she shouldn't know.

And even as she did, her mind whirled. She looked up, the light from the moon sliding through the blinds and hitting his face just right, in a way that almost made her scream again—this time for a far different reason.

She knew him.

She couldn't know him.

But she did.

Her body shook, though not from the way he'd fucked her; from the realization that everything had changed, and not for the better. Then he came, screaming the letter she was known by because she hadn't given him her full name.

And she wouldn't.

Ever.

There should have been no names tonight. There never were before. Those were the rules. The boundaries that had been set to ensure that no one got hurt.

And yet it was all a lie.

Because she knew his name.

She knew his face.

And in that one brief moment when the light had hit his eyes just right, and she had seen the boy he had been instead of the man he was, she knew that the fragile peace she'd thought she had collected was a sham.

He was the one person she wasn't supposed to have. The one she knew could break her, shatter it all.

So she knew that when the time came to meet again, she'd have to walk away. She'd have to end what they had even though she was positive it would ruin a part of her.

She couldn't undo the fragile trust they'd created through their promises and touch. If she stayed, if she came back, she'd be the liar she'd always told herself she would never become.

This was the boy she'd fallen in love with before she knew what love was beyond cupcakes and butterflies. This was the man that she had tested her boundaries with. And now, it seemed he was the man she'd truly tested fate with.

Because this man was a stranger with a familiar face. He was someone from her past who she had sworn to forget.

Someone who could break her.

This was Derek.

The man she needed to forget.

And the one person Olivia knew she wouldn't.

Chapter Two

Derek Hawkins hovered above the woman he only knew as O and held back a frown at the expression on her face. This wasn't the look of a woman sated and worn out from a long night of sex. No, she looked as if she'd seen a ghost and wanted to be anywhere but where she was.

And considering that he was buried balls-deep inside her, the condom still warm from his come, he wasn't feeling so pleased with that fact. Her tight pussy was currently wrapped around his dick, her inner walls clamping down on him in waves as she came down from her own orgasm. All of this was happening as she looked at him but didn't meet his eyes.

Why the fuck wouldn't she meet his eyes?

He shifted slightly, still inside her, and traced his finger along her cheekbone. When she didn't lean into his touch, didn't look at him, he knew something was wrong.

Had he hurt her? Had they gone too fast, had he been too rough? They'd gone harder before, faster even, but maybe he'd missed a cue somewhere? He quickly pulled out of her, ditched the condom on the side table thanks to some convenient tissues, and checked her over.

"What's wrong? Did I hurt you?" He hated the way his need for her bled into his voice. They weren't a couple, weren't anything except two people who respected one another and had fun even though they kept their distance. He liked what they had, even if part of him wanted more, and still another part knew he needed to walk away before he hurt her. But that didn't mean he'd let himself hurt her now.

She turned her head to the side and looked at him, confusion on her face. For some reason, that settled him down more than anything she could have said.

"No, of course, you didn't hurt me. You never hurt me. I like what we do." She cleared her throat and sat up, pulling the sheet up with her. Somehow, during their first round, they'd tossed the comforter down to the floor and had slid under the sheets. That didn't always happen since they usually went at it against a wall or on another piece of furniture first, but this time, they'd gone for the bed.

He didn't like the fact that she'd covered herself with the damn sheet, though. He liked seeing her dark nipples and light brown skin completely bare. Yeah, the contrast of the cream sheets against her darker skin was hot as hell, but he still didn't like that she felt as if she needed to cover herself up.

"Then why won't you meet my eyes? I know you came, but didn't you like what we did?" He hated how insecure he sounded, but he was just coming down from his own high, and he wasn't thinking clearly. He never thought clearly when it came to O.

And fuck, he'd asked her to call him Derek, demanded it more like. He *wanted* her to know him, wanted to know who she was. He was getting too old for their game, and from what he knew of O, he liked her.

But he had a feeling he'd changed the game and not for the better, and now he was probably going to get screwed over—and not in a good way—because he'd taken that step.

She turned then, meeting his gaze full on for the first time since they'd gotten into bed. "I think I need to go."

He blinked. "Was it because I asked you to call me Derek? I figured after all this time, a first name would be okay. Though you never told me yours." He paused. "Are you going to?"

"We've had fun…Derek. But I think this needs to be the last time. The last month." She slowly slid out of bed and started pulling on her clothes. All Derek could do was stand there, naked, his dick still wet, and his hands fisted at his sides.

She was hiding something from him. Not just her name, but something…else, and he wanted to know what. He wanted to know *her*. And now she was running? Wasn't that just his damn luck? As soon as he decided he wanted more, she decided to run away.

Of course.

"You're kidding, right? We've been doing this…how long? How many years? What happened that made you change your mind?"

Once again, she didn't meet his eyes, but she did turn, her back exposed, and he let out a curse. Without words, he went to zip up her dress, annoyed with himself for doing so. He wasn't an asshole, was far from it according to his friends, but he felt like one now. He wanted to growl and yell and make her tell him what was wrong. But he knew that wasn't going to help anything, and if he wasn't careful, she'd walk right out of this room tonight and out of his life forever.

The thing was, he had a feeling she just might do that anyway.

And there was nothing he could do about it.

When she turned in his arms, he had to hold back from sucking in a breath. He always did when it came to her. She was so damn beautiful with her dark hair tumbling down her back, her wide eyes, and her light brown skin that was so damn soft he could caress her for hours. *Had* touched her for hours.

"Thank you," she whispered. "I always forget to wear a wrap dress or something without a zipper for you."

"I like undressing you," he said honestly. "I thought you liked it when I did."

She let out a sigh. "I do. I did. But this needs to be the last time. I'm sorry, Derek. I just…I need to go."

She moved to walk around him, and because he knew he was a big dude and tended to crowd people even when he didn't mean to, he took a step out of the way so she could grab her bag.

"So this is it? I tell you my name, and now you're done. Because I thought what we had was good."

"It was good. But now, our time is over. Don't you think we should move on? Find something that's not…this? What we are. We're not getting any younger."

If he didn't hear the emotion in her voice, didn't hear the fact that she sounded as if she were about to fucking cry, he'd have called her cold. But she was leaving for a reason, and she apparently wasn't going to tell him what that was.

And he had no idea what to do to find out.

Fuck.

"At least tell me your name. That's all I ask." It's all he could ask for, though not all he wanted to request.

She met his eyes again, and this time, he swore he should have known more just from that look alone, but he knew he was missing something.

"Olivia."

He let out a breath. He should have known she'd be an Olivia. The name fit her perfectly, but he still didn't know why she was leaving.

"I'm coming back next month," he said quickly. "Even if you aren't here, I'm coming back. Because I like what we have and I don't want it to end."

"But we have to stop," she whispered.

Have to. Not want to. But she wasn't going to tell him why. Didn't matter if he deserved an answer, he wasn't going to get one.

Then she went on her toes, kissed his jaw, and walked out of the hotel room, leaving him standing naked, cold, and shocked to his core.

He finally knew her name, and now she was gone. Maybe forever.

And he had no idea what the fuck he was going to do about it.

Derek punched the bag in front of him, pissed off and muttering to himself, low enough that the rest of the gym couldn't hear him.

"That wasn't our bargain," he growled with another punch. Anger coursed through his veins, and he forced himself to keep his form so he wouldn't hurt himself. His hands were his business, and screwing them up because he was angry and hurt would only piss him off more.

He'd left the hotel soon after Olivia, making sure he picked up all their things. She hadn't even left a single earring behind when she'd run like the hounds of hell were on her tail. He'd checked out of the room, ignoring the knowing look from the overnight clerk that he hadn't met before. Then, he'd gone home and tossed and turned all night, thinking of what he could have done differently.

He liked O, Olivia, wanted to know more about her. He liked their relationship, or whatever it was they had. He liked knowing that once a month he'd go to the hotel where he first met her, and they'd have each other for those few short hours. She was not only the best sex he'd ever had, but he also liked her smile, her laugh, and the way her eyes danced when they flirted.

And while part of him had always wanted to know more about her, he also liked the safe distance they kept between the two of them. Their deal had been the longest relationship he'd ever had. The fact that he hadn't had another person in his life over the last four years might have been because of her, or it might have been because of his own issues. He had enough on his plate without adding someone with strings and commitments who would need to rely on him for things he couldn't give.

And yet he'd been able to commit in his own weird way when it came to Olivia.

He'd shown up every month for four goddamn years, and she'd always been there. It had been the healthiest, longest commitment he'd ever made, and yet it hadn't actually been a commitment at all.

And then she'd just walked away because she was done.

He couldn't help but blame himself. He must have done something, said something. Maybe telling her his name had made it all too real. Maybe she'd needed the fantasy more than he had. He didn't know, but now, all he could do was hope to hell that she showed up next month.

He had a feeling that these next four weeks would be hell on his nerves.

"Hell." He let his fist fly one last time before hitting the showers. He usually worked out after work so his hands weren't sore, but he'd been stressed out and needed some form of release that didn't have anything to do with his fist wrapped around his dick.

By the time he headed into work and parked behind the shop in their tiny private lot, he was still on edge and knew his friends and coworkers weren't going to let him get out of telling them what was on his mind.

The problem with working at Montgomery Ink was that everyone was not only great at what they did, but they were also close enough to be family. And while only two were family by blood, the rest had enough connections that they always knew when something was up with one of the others.

Derek himself had been on the offering end of that help over the years. When his friends had needed assistance in their love lives or had needed someone to talk to, he'd been there. Somehow, he'd found the right words and had been one of the steady forces in the shop.

And now he had a feeling that as soon as he walked in, he wouldn't be able to hide his frustration or whatever else was wrong with him thanks to O.

Olivia.

Jesus, he needed to get her out of his head and only think about her in four weeks when he hoped to hell she showed up. Maybe she'd just gotten scared about knowing more about him, but neither of them had missed a night in four years, and he hoped that they wouldn't start now despite what she'd said. Because she hadn't given him a real reason, and maybe that meant she didn't have one.

Maybe she'd come back.

And maybe he was an idiot and needed to get over this woman he didn't know as well as he probably should have.

Any hope of hiding his reactions to the previous night ended as soon as he walked in and found one of his bosses leaning against the front desk, her pierced brow raised as she got a look at him.

"Why do you look like you were hung up wet and left to dry?" Maya asked as she tapped her finger on the desk.

Derek would have flipped her off, but then she'd really know something was wrong. Instead, he just gave her a slow blink and went back to his station. She snorted, and he had a feeling there was no way he'd get out of whatever conversation she wanted to have, but first, he hoped he'd at least be able to get his workstation set up.

Montgomery Ink was one of—if not *the*—hottest tattoo shops in Denver. Most of the artists, including him, had waiting lists over a year long. His bosses, siblings Austin and Maya, were even opening up another shop down in Colorado Springs with their cousins, who would own the building and run the place from there. Derek had no clue how talented and business-savvy the crew was until he found himself working with some of the best in the tattooing world.

There had even been talk of a reality series following the crew around, but Austin and Maya had been quick to shut that down. Their family was a large one, and they'd all been through hell over the past few years. Now, all eight siblings were either married or on their way to being hitched, and most of them had children. They just wanted to settle down and do what they loved. In fact, almost every member of Montgomery Ink, even those without the Montgomery surname, was married and planning a family.

Only Derek and Brandon were left, but he had a feeling from what had happened a couple of days ago at the shop when that stranger who didn't seem to be a stranger to his friend had shown up, that Brandon wouldn't be single for long.

That left Derek. The guy who had all the advice because he'd been through a lot in his life, but the one who didn't have a wife or girlfriend of his own.

And that meant that everyone would want to *help* him. They'd already tried setting him up on dates or asking what his type of woman was, and he'd done his best to put a stop to that. Now, though, with his lack of sleep and genuine confusion over what had happened the night before with Olivia, he had no idea what he was going to do.

Sighing, he went to work getting ready for his first client of the day. They didn't open for another hour, so he had time to set up and get a cup of coffee from the café next door. However, before he could even get up to go over there, Sloane, the artist next to him, who happened to be married to the café owner next door, pulled up a seat beside Derek, a hazelnut latte in his hand.

Derek's favorite.

Hailey, Sloane's wife, knew everyone's drink order—their favorites or if they were in the mood for something different—without having to ask. It was spooky, and yet he loved it.

However, if Sloane was here with the drink, that meant that Maya had already told Hailey that something was up, and they were starting with the big guns—literally in Sloane's case since the man was built like a brick shithouse.

"Thanks."

Sloane grunted. "I don't talk about feelings. But you look like shit, and we have time to talk. So, spill."

Maya, who stood behind Sloane, cracked up. "Smooth."

Sloane shrugged. "We open soon, and there's no time for beating around the bush."

"I like the way you think," Austin said from Maya's other side. The shop had filled when Derek was setting up. Austin, Blake, Maya, Sloane, Callie, Brandon, and Jax were all there, watching.

The shop hadn't been this full in a while since they usually didn't work all at once, but now that they'd remodeled a bit, there was more room. However, this meant that every single artist was staring at him.

"What?" he finally said.

"Don't 'what' us," Maya put in. "You look sad. And, usually, when you go out for your date or whatever the hell you call it, you come back looking all lubed up."

"Jesus Christ," Austin muttered under his breath, and the rest of the crew laughed.

"Lubed up?" Derek asked.

"It's true," Maya said.

Then Maya's words caught up with him. "Wait. How the hell do you know about my dates?"

"You got drunk and mentioned it to Sloane once," Callie said. She grinned at him through her multicolored hair, and he wanted to close his eyes and growl.

Sloane had the decency to wince. "And then I mentioned it to Hailey since I was also drunk and forgot to tell her not to tell Maya."

"And now that I know, the people who matter know because we love you and want you happy. But why aren't you happy?"

"I'm fine."

"You aren't," Jax put in. He was their newest artist but had fit in quickly.

"I'll *be* fine. How's that?"

"Why don't you just tell us what's up and then we can move on?" Austin said quickly, clearly ready for this conversation to be done. As Derek wanted the same and knew he couldn't get out of it, he decided he'd just get it over with. He had no idea what he was doing, after all; maybe they could help.

"I met a girl a few years ago. A woman. We're having fun. Or we were. We meet up once a month at the same place, have a good night, and don't talk to or see each other until the next month. No names, no numbers, nothing is shared except the experience. It's nice. It's different. She's nice. She's different. But now she says she doesn't want to do it anymore, and I have no idea what's going on. I'm still going to show up next month, you know. Because I can't just let it end, but it's not like I know what to do other than that."

He hadn't realized he'd blurted it all out until he looked up and the crew was staring at him like he'd grown another head. Maybe he had because he sure as hell didn't feel like himself just then.

"I have more questions, but we don't have time for explanations of why and how," Callie put in. "But do you like her? Do you want to see her more than just the one night a month? Because if you do, find her."

"I can't find her. That was the whole point of our arrangement."

"Then wait for a month and see if she shows up," Sloane said. "Just don't stalk her or some shit and be that creepy asshole we have to beat up."

"Amen," Brandon and Jax said at the same time before smirking at each other.

"I'm not going to fucking stalk her. But I want to know why she wants to end it. Does she want more and think I don't? Did she find someone else? I want to know *why,* and I don't want to wait, but I think I have to."

"Do you have a photo of her?" Maya asked. "Maybe we know her. We know a lot of people."

Derek gave her a dry look. "We live in Denver, not some Podunk town. I don't think you know her."

"At least let us see," Callie pleaded. "If you have a pic that is."

"I have one," he mumbled and dug out his phone. They each had one photo of each other, though it hadn't been part of their terms. He hadn't been able to help himself and looked at the damn thing often. She was wearing just a sheet, but you couldn't tell unless you knew and he was glad about that. The look in her eyes, the parting of her lips was just for him.

And now he was going to share her, at least this small part of her, and he wasn't sure he wanted to. But he wasn't sure he could hold back if he wanted to find her.

He flipped his phone around, and while the guys grinned, Callie and Maya gave each other cats in cream looks. And then Austin cursed under his breath.

"What?" Derek asked. "You know her?" There was no way that could be true, no way fate could be that kind to him after all the kicks and wounds it had given him over the years.

"Yeah, I know her. That's Olivia. My neighbor." Austin shook his head. "Has to mean something, man."

Derek just sat there, pulling his phone back so he could look at her again. Did it? Did it mean something? Because if she were truly Austin's neighbor, then maybe he had a second chance.

Or maybe everything had been doomed from the start, and he needed to give her the space she wanted. But what he did know was that it wasn't over, not by a long shot.

Fate seemed to be on his side for once, and he wasn't going to let that go. Not this time.

Not again.

Chapter Three

Olivia had a headache from hell, and she only wished it had been from drinking the night before. As she tended not to drink while she was home since she wasn't a huge fan of drinking alone, that meant her pain came from work stress and lack of sleep.

It had been two days since she'd last seen Derek, her D, and she couldn't get him off her mind. Hell, she hadn't been able to get him off her mind for over twenty years when he was her Derek, and then again for four more years as her D. How was she supposed to not think of him at all when he was both?

"Ugh." She ran her hand down her face, willing her mind to stay on the correct subject rather than one she should have pushed into the secret vault of her mind long ago. If only Derek hadn't said his name, if only she hadn't noticed his eyes in just the right light when he said it, she might not have put everything together. Honestly, she didn't know how she hadn't realized who he was for so long, but it must have been for a reason. Her mind and memories had given her a reprieve only to come back full force and slap her in the face with vicious taunts and accusations.

It didn't matter that those jabs were from her and not Derek. They were still there no matter what, and she couldn't forget about them.

Damn it. She had work to do, a person to forget, and a life to try and get through. Dwelling on a man she couldn't see again, a man she *wouldn't* see again, wouldn't help anything.

But it didn't mean that her mind was actually going to let that happen. She was Olivia, after all, the person who fixated on one thing and worried herself to the point of exhaustion and confusion over it.

"I need to work," she whispered to herself, aware that if anyone were home with her, they'd think she was talking to herself. The fact that she was actually talking to herself was of no consequence. She was a freelance editor. She *always* talked to herself. And if that wasn't a ringing endorsement for her sanity and her services, she didn't know what was.

With a sigh, she opened her document and tried to get into the moment of the book. Her current project was content editing the first book in a new romance trilogy, and she was already in love with the story. This was her third time working with this particular author, and they were starting to really create a routine.

Of course, even as she said that, she did her best not to cringe at the note she had to write. The author had decided to kill a momma cat in order to bring the vet heroine and the grumpy hero together. It totally made sense and was well done, but Olivia knew that one of the rules in romance was that you didn't kill the pets. Her rules started with an HEA, so no killing heroes or heroines and no cheating. And then the pet rule.

Olivia hoped the author would be up for changing that aspect because she didn't want this author's readers to get upset and put her on a *list,* and now she kind of hated herself for even putting the note in at all. The scene was done perfectly and worked with the book, but…there were rules.

Rules.

Of course, there were rules. There were for everything. And Olivia had broken all of them where Derek and D were concerned.

Yes, she was thinking of them as two different people since she had different guidelines for each of them, but now they were all mixed up in her mind, and she thought she might be sick. No wonder her brain hurt.

Olivia sipped her coffee, wincing since it was cold, but she was too lazy to get up and make another cup. That and she was a firm believer that if she made it, she had to drink it, cool or not. Hence why she drank caramel coffee because it tasted better cold than regular coffee and she tended to get lost in work or her thoughts enough that cold coffee was part of her daily routine.

She had a few more hours on this content edit and then she could send it back to the author before starting her next project, which was a copyedit since she was certified in that, too. She liked switching between the two so her brain could stay fresh for the next round, and she was grateful that her job let her work from home while she did it. She'd fallen into the gig, and she loved it.

Not only did she get to read some amazing work from talented authors but she also got to work in cute leggings and tanks with balconette bras rather than ones with wires. She didn't need to wear makeup or shoes, and more often than not, she ended up with her hair piled on top of her head with her blue-tinted reading glasses sliding down the bridge of her nose.

Yep, she loved her job.

It was the other aspects of her life that left a bit to be desired lately, apparently.

Annoyed with herself for getting off track once more thanks to a mistake she wouldn't be making again, she pushed the object of her distraction out of her mind and went back to work. She was so involved in the heroine's journey that she let out a tiny scream when her phone rang.

She'd forgotten that she'd turned up the volume for her alarm and hadn't reset it, and quickly put the phone back to vibrate before answering.

"Hey, Alice." Alice was her best friend though she lived in another state and usually didn't call during the day since they were both working. So if she was calling, it was either important, or she was stuck on a scene. Her friend was an author and one of her clients and usually wrote all day and plotted at night. Olivia had always admired the other woman for her creativity because while Olivia loved editing, she knew she would never be an author and she was just fine with that.

"I hate this book."

Olivia snorted since Alice sounded serious, but her friend got to this point in her work at least once a project, and it was Olivia's job to calm the other woman down. The two had only met once in real life but they talked almost daily. Alice was a few inches taller than Olivia, far more slender, and her skin was a few shades darker. When the two had met at a conference, according to Alice, they'd turned heads since, apparently, they made a sexy picture. Olivia, as usual, hadn't noticed. But that's why she had Alice. One of the many reasons.

"You always say that, and then you end up loving the book. You're at the middle, aren't you?"

"Why do books even need a middle? Why can't it just begin, they have sex, and then boom, ending? Those are so much easier to write."

"And yet you come to me while you're looking at a blank page, asking why books need a beginning. And then again at the ending where you say you just want to blow everything up or throw them into bed and call it a day. I know how you work, missy."

"Don't throw my words back in my face. I'm not supposed to make any sense. I'm an author."

They both laughed, and Olivia sank back into her chair, her head still throbbing but not as much as before. She was going to count that as progress.

"You're a dork. But that's why I love you."

"I love you, too. But why is writing so hard? I mean, we're in what century now? Why can't we just plug our brains into our computer and just get all of our thoughts right out of our minds and onto the screen?"

"You say that, but I've seen a movie with that plot, and it didn't end well for the humans."

"Well, it would if it were my books. It's all angst and intrigue with steamy sex and a happily ever after. The world needs more happily ever afters."

That was the truth. And, of course, on that thought, Derek once again slipped into Olivia's mind, and she did her best not to think too hard about him. Some part of her had once thought that their once-a-month meetings could perhaps be something more. Another part of her had thought that keeping it at once a month kept her safe.

She'd been wrong on both counts because she was never going to see him again. Not when she could hurt him by making him remember.

She'd already hurt herself by doing that.

"You there, Olivia?"

Alice's voice brought her out of her thoughts, and she cleared her throat. "Sorry. Just thinking."

"You're always thinking. Same as me. And while we occasionally trail off mid-sentence because we're in our heads, I don't think that was the case this time. What's wrong?"

That was the problem when your best friend knew you so well. Alice tended to know Olivia's moods before she did. The fact that Alice could do that without knowing Olivia's past spoke well of Alice's talents, but Olivia wasn't going to share everything, not yet. She needed to tend to her own thoughts and figure out what she was going to do about these new revelations before she shared anything with Alice.

"Nothing's wrong. Just thinking about work." A lie. And she hated herself for it, but she wasn't ready to tell Alice everything.

She wasn't sure if she ever would be.

"I know that's not one hundred percent true, but I'm going to let it slide because you know as soon as you're ready to talk about it, I'm here. You and I do best when we don't push each other and know our boundaries."

Olivia let out a relieved sigh, aware that Alice could hear it as well. She loved the other woman, and what she loved most about her was that she respected Olivia's need for privacy. She did the same for Alice, and that was why the two of them worked so well as friends.

"Thanks."

"No problem. And now I have an idea for the middle part of the book. Talk to you later."

Olivia didn't even have a chance to say goodbye before Alice was off the phone and onto her book. That was her friend, completely in the zone when she wanted to be even if she was a distraction from Olivia's work at the same time. It was okay, though, because her watch buzzed at that moment, reminding her to move. Her job required her to sit for long periods of time, staring at a computer—and ruining her body in the process.

She would just go for a walk, clear her head, and then come back to finish up the end. If she focused, she could finish today and get the book out well ahead of time. That was always her favorite thing to do, but she also did her best not to get authors used to that in case she got behind, or the book took longer than expected. The latter usually happened with fantasy books because the world was so vivid she either got lost in it or had to break it apart to make sure it flowed. She loved it, but it was even more of a headache than the one currently running rampant through her brain.

After making sure she'd hit save one more time on her project, she closed her laptop and went to her bedroom to find her shoes. Since she was already wearing leggings and a tank, she was pretty much always ready to work out. Not that she wore them for that reason, but the practicality of not having to change was nice. She couldn't run in the bra she was wearing, but with the size of her breasts, it took two sports bras at a minimum to keep herself from bruising her chin.

She was pretty sure it had happened once, and explaining boob strain and bruised chins to people wasn't something she ever wanted to do.

Not again.

She pulled on a light jacket and made her way outside, putting in her headphones so she could listen to an audiobook rather than hearing the sound of her feet hitting the pavement. If she had to listen to that, then she wouldn't walk, and she'd end up lazing about, working and slowly growing horizontally. If she were ever to run— something she only did when she contemplated the zombie apocalypse and reminded herself that she needed to at least be fast enough to outrun them—she had to put on loud music rather than a book.

Olivia was a little kooky, but she was fine with that. She'd long since realized she'd be the crazy cat lady living alone as she worked at home. She just needed a cat—something she was going to do soon, but she hadn't found the right one at the shelter yet. Plus, she was still getting over losing her other cat last year and didn't want to bring about change so quickly.

And now she was walking quickly and blinking away tears while trying not to think of her cat *or* Derek.

She was officially losing her mind.

With a deep breath, she focused on her audiobook while making her one-mile trip around the neighborhood. Any more than that, and she got bored, so she took more than one walk a day. How she'd become so neurotic, she didn't know, but it worked for her.

On her last leg, she passed her neighbor's house and smiled, waving as Sierra Montgomery got into her SUV with her two sons, Leif and Colin. Leif was as tall as Sierra now, and Olivia wasn't sure how that had happened. She'd been living next to Sierra's husband, Austin, for years, even before he met and married Sierra and before Leif, his son from a previous relationship, had shown up. She didn't know the whole story as it wasn't her business, but she knew the family was a loving one.

She also knew that Austin had like seven siblings who were all married and most had kids of their own. Sometimes, Austin had the entire crew over for a family event, and Sierra would always come over with leftovers or even a whole cake, apologizing for the noise. Olivia never minded since everyone was always nice to her and they were never loud after nine at night. She'd had worse neighbors. The Montgomerys were actually pretty amazing. Plus, Austin always came over to help her fix things she couldn't reach. She might not have a man in her life, but she had friends and acquaintances who helped out when things were beyond her abilities.

Before Sierra drove off, Austin came outside, gave Olivia a curious look, and then went to kiss his wife. Olivia's heart melted a tad, and she held back a swoon as Sierra took a staggering step backward before getting into her SUV. The man could apparently kiss, and after all their years of marriage, the two were still pretty damn hot.

Olivia was only a little jealous.

And by a little, she meant a lot.

Olivia went to sit on her porch and enjoy some of the breeze before she headed back inside, so she was in Austin's line of sight as another car pulled into the space Sierra had just vacated. Since the couple constantly had family and friends from the tattoo shop visiting, this wasn't a surprise.

What *was* a surprise was the man who got out of the vehicle, his long legs encased in jeans that made his thighs look sexy as hell. He had on a thin Henley that only enhanced his broad shoulders and trim waist. His beard was growing in and made her want to run her fingers through it, and his hair was brushed back out of his face, though she knew he needed a haircut.

Derek.

Holy hell.

Austin knew Derek.

She fought to control her breathing as Austin and Derek did that man hug that always confused her before Austin turned to her, a brow raised.

Traitor.

She didn't know why that thought popped into her head, or how Austin knew Derek, or even how Derek knew that Austin knew her.

All she knew was that the man she needed to stay away from was currently walking toward her—far too sexily—with an intense look in his eyes. He actually *prowled,* and all she could think was that he was the predator and she was the prey.

Only, in the end, he would be the one that got hurt. She knew it.

After all, she would deliver the final blow.

Again.

Chapter Four

Derek knew he should take it slow, maybe even so slow that he didn't go to her right away. He should walk into Austin's house and let Olivia have her space, all the while knowing that she would be able to reach him if she needed to.

Only he didn't do that.

He'd never claimed to be a smart man, after all.

He couldn't help but notice her wide eyes set in her always expressive face. Her hair was piled on top of her head, and she wore tight leggings that showcased her curves.

Curves he'd touched, licked, and bitten multiple times over the years.

He held back a groan and willed his cock to behave. He wanted to keep her in his life, and going to her house unannounced with a hard-on wasn't the way to do it. He already felt like he was verging on stalker territory so he would have to tread lightly.

"Hey, Olivia."

She swallowed hard, and he watched her throat work. She didn't move from her seat, and he had no idea what that meant.

"You're…you're here."

He stood on Austin's side of the yard, not going onto her property. He didn't want to come near her if she didn't want him there, so he was being damn careful not to encroach.

"I am. I know it's weird and not what either of us said we'd do, but I was at work, and the subject of you came up. And, well, apparently Austin knew you. Small world, right?"

She didn't say anything, but her breathing quickened. It took all of his power not to look at the rise and fall of her generous breasts because he was, well...him, and he liked the look of her. But he also didn't want her to kick him out of her line of sight and call the cops. Not that she would, but still.

"I asked Austin if I could come over and talk to you. I didn't ask for your number since it wasn't Austin's to give. And I'm still on Austin's property, so I'm not on yours making you feel uncomfortable. Too much. Or at least I'm trying not to. If you want me to go, I will. But I want to talk to you, O. Let me talk to you."

She was quiet for so long that he was afraid he'd fucked up and feared she'd run. Since she'd already done that and he didn't know why, he just stood there, his hands by his sides as he tried to look non-threatening. He was a big man with a beard, longish hair, and tattoos, so that wasn't the easiest thing for him to do.

"I can't believe you're here."

"I can't believe you're Austin's neighbor. But it must be for a reason, right?"

Her face shut down, and she bit her lip. "Not everything connected is for a good reason, D—Derek."

He didn't know what she meant by that, but she stood up and rested her hands on her hips.

"We won't do anything you don't want to do. I promise."

She met his eyes and gave him a slight nod. He didn't know why the overwhelming rush of relief slammed into him, but he was damn happy that she was giving him a chance. He didn't know what he wanted from her or himself for that matter, but he knew if he walked away, it would be over.

And he didn't want it to be over.

Whatever *it* was.

"I guess you should come in." She was silent for a moment as if she were collecting her thoughts, and hell, he was doing the same. "There are things we should talk about."

He gave her a tight nod and took a step across the invisible boundary line that separated Austin's and Olivia's properties. Austin had already gone inside his house when Derek had moved away without a word—he'd heard the door close behind him. Austin would understand the need for privacy more than most, though the man was probably ready to come out if Olivia needed help. Hell, Austin might be Derek's friend, but Derek didn't mind that Austin would be on Olivia's side—if there were even sides in this case. After all, Derek would do the same.

Derek watched her move as he followed her into her home. He still couldn't quite believe how things had all worked out, and he had a feeling that this was only the beginning. He wished he knew what he wanted, but all he knew for sure was that he didn't want what they had to end. He'd talk to her, see what she had to say, and inquire if she wanted to meet again next month. He wouldn't pressure her, wouldn't push her into an uncomfortable situation, but he knew that what they had was too good to let go so easily.

They were more than just one night a month, that much he knew. How much more, however, was something they would have to figure out together. That was, if she let him back into her life, even if for a single night a month again.

When she closed the door behind him, he glanced around her home, trying to get a sense of who this Olivia was. He hadn't even known her full first name until their last night together, and though he'd always known that was what they'd promised themselves and each other, part of him had wanted more. He'd thought he knew more about her than he did because of how close they were when they were together for their one night a month. He'd learned every part of her—every deep intake of breath, every curve, every soft touch—yet that hadn't been enough. And while he liked the way she smiled, the way she made him laugh, the way she held nothing back except for who they were when they were together, he didn't know anything else about her.

And the thought that he might never see her again had just brought the idea to him that he needed more of her, needed more than a single night.

He needed her.

Hell, that might be too much for even him so quickly, but he'd told himself that he just needed to see her again so he could figure out what the hell he was going to do. He was turning himself into knots as he circled around what the hell his brain and heart wanted, and yet he wasn't accomplishing anything.

Derek wasn't an asshole, and it was about time he started acting like the man he was when he was around her. His O, his Olivia.

Her home was decent-sized, not as big as Austin's since the other man's house was a little farther back off the road with a longer driveway so he had more room to build, but Olivia's house seemed to suit her—at least the parts of her he knew and the pieces of the home he saw. She had light colors on the walls and light rugs over dark, hardwood floors. Everything looked to be in place and dusted, as if she took care of what she owned and didn't have children or a pet to knock things over.

He didn't even know if she had a kid or a pet. How could he not know those things? He knew she wasn't married only because that was one of their agreements when they'd first started their arrangement. Neither of them wanted to end up being a cheater, so they'd laid out the fact that they weren't married early on.

None of the photos on the walls featured men, and Austin had even said that Olivia lived alone, so that much about her was true.

But what else had he been missing when he was burying his head in the sand and the feeling of just being with her?

"This is weird," Olivia said under her breath, and he turned to look at her. She had her hands folded in front of her, her eyes wide. Her teeth kept biting into those lips that he loved to nibble on himself.

He stuck his hands into the pockets of his jeans and rocked back on his heels. "Yeah, I guess it is. I've never seen you without a slinky dress on."

She grinned. "As I'm currently wearing yoga pants and no makeup, it makes up a different picture altogether, doesn't it?"

Since he liked seeing the shape of her ass and thighs in those yoga pants, he wasn't going to complain. "You look sexy no matter what you wear. Not going to lie about that. And I like you with and without makeup. I'm not one of those guys who's going to say which one he prefers since it's not about what I like, it's about what you like. Plus, you're beyond beautiful either way."

Her eyes widened even more, and she blinked quickly. "Oh. Well, that's nice to hear. Most guys are jerks about things like that even when they think they're being sophisticated by saying something that contradicts that entirely."

"I still can't believe you're Austin's neighbor."

"How…how do you know Austin, exactly? Because it's weird that you know him. You know?"

He nodded, not taking a step closer to her, knowing they both might need space to keep their thoughts in order. The problem when he was near her was that he always wanted to touch her, and that didn't make for easy thinking.

"I'm a tattoo artist at Montgomery Ink. I used to be a floater and would come in every month from a different city as I tried to get my credentials in order and build my portfolio. But you knew when I was in town since that time always coincided with *our* time."

She didn't say anything, but he didn't really expect her to. There wasn't much to say about the idea that they had an unusual arrangement—especially now that she wanted it to end.

He just hoped she didn't really mean that.

"Now I'm here in Denver full-time. I used to live here when I was younger, moved away after school, and am finally here to stay. Austin and Maya, the owners of the shop, hired me on full-time, so now I have a steady income and all that." He didn't know why he was rambling, but hell, he had no idea what he should say to her.

How did he tell a woman that he still wanted her in his bed and wanted to see what they could possibly be outside of it, all the while knowing he might not ever be ready for a real commitment?

He'd lost a part of himself years ago when it came to someone he loved, and he wasn't sure he could ever let himself feel what he needed in a relationship. Maybe he was a selfish bastard when it came to Olivia, but he couldn't stop himself from wanting her, wanting more.

And that was the problem.

"They're a good crew. Austin did some of my ink in the past."

As Derek had licked over that ink, he'd admired the work, thought it looked familiar, and now he knew why. Small world.

"They're the best. I'm just glad they let me stay." He was silent a bit longer as he tried to think about what to say, what he wanted to say. He was good with words when it came to other people, but with himself and his own needs and desires? He was beyond lacking in that department.

Maybe if he could get his head around what he actually wanted, he'd be able to say what he needed to, but that wasn't going to happen anytime soon.

Worry covered her face, and he stepped forward, cupping her cheeks between his hands before he thought better of it.

"What's wrong?"

"I...I can't believe you're here."

"I can't either."

"There are things I need to tell you."

He nodded, his eyes on hers but not truly hearing the words. He was so damn selfish when it came to Olivia, and he knew it.

"Later."

And because he couldn't help himself, he kissed her, needing her touch more than the air he breathed. When she put her hands on his chest, he was afraid that she might push him away, but she didn't.

Instead, she kept her palms on him, not pushing or pulling, just resting, so he took that as an agreement. He deepened the kiss, his hands sliding through her hair as he pressed her back gently against the door. She moaned into him, and he pulled away slightly so he could bite down on her lip where she had before. When she let out a slight gasp, he licked over the sting and then sucked, loving the way her eyes darkened.

He kissed down her neck to her shoulder, tugging the strap of her bra over slightly so he could reach the spot on her skin that always made her shudder beneath his touch. He knew this part of her, knew so damn much, but yet he knew it wasn't enough. Because there was more to life than great sex, and though he and Olivia had the best of it, he wanted more from her and with her.

Hadn't he wanted more when he told her to call him Derek? That had been the trigger, he knew. The reason she'd pushed him away. And he needed to find out the why of it. Once he pulled away, once he was able to think clearly and not keep kissing and tasting her skin like he was currently doing, he'd be able to ask her, be able to find out more about her.

But he couldn't stop his hands from going down her curves to cup her breasts, molding them in his big palms. And, yeah, he had big hands, but her generous tits overfilled them. He fucking *loved* that. He loved sliding his dick between them in the hotel shower as he fucked her tits and how she would lower her head to suck on the tip of his dick. It was always so damn sexy, and she was the one who usually initiated it since she liked it, too. Then he'd suck and bite on her nipples until she came without him even touching her pussy. He'd heard that was hard to do with women with larger breasts since, apparently, their nipples weren't as sensitive in most cases, but not when it came to his Olivia.

He groaned at the memory of two months ago when he'd fucked her tits for the final time. He'd come on her skin, pearly liquid flowing down her breasts and over her nipples until he was spent. Then he washed her fully, making her come again with his hands and mouth.

They'd both been exhausted by the end of it and had curled up in bed together, only to wake a couple of hours later and make love again.

And then the two of them had parted ways, their only promise that there was to be no promises other than a month's gap in time.

Things had changed this last time, and as he kissed her again now, rocking his hips into hers, he knew that things had changed yet again. He just didn't know what they were going to do about it. That was why they needed to talk. Why he needed to pull his mouth and hands away from her and actually *listen*.

He needed to stop being such a selfish dick.

So he pulled away, breathing heavily along with her as he rested his forehead on hers. "That…that is something we've always been good at."

She seemed to shrink in on herself at his words, and he leaned back, worried that he'd hurt her. "Olivia? Did I fuck up? What's wrong?"

She shook her head. "No, you didn't. I need to talk to you, though. I really, really do before you kiss me again and before I let you kiss me."

Worry crept up his spine, and he was about to say that they should head to the living room and sit down so she could tell him what could possibly put that look in her eyes, but his phone buzzed a familiar pattern, and he let out a curse.

"Shit, I'm sorry, it's my mom. I can't let it go to voicemail." He had reasons for that, but they were far too complicated to tell Olivia just then.

She seemed to pale even more but gave him a tight nod as he

answered.

"Mom?"

"I need you to come to the house." Her voice was a shallow rasp, and he knew he didn't have much time to get to her. He never did.

"I'll be there as soon as I can. Just lay down. Okay?"

She didn't answer, but she never did. Not since…well, not since their world had changed, and Derek had lost what he'd thought was his future. He hung up and put his phone back into his pocket.

"I've got to go. My mom needs me." He shook his head at Olivia's look. "I'll explain one day." He hoped. Maybe.

"I understand." And for some reason, he thought maybe she did, but he didn't know how she could. "Just…there's something I need to tell you."

He kissed her hard one more time. "Okay." She let out a relieved breath. "Next month." When she stiffened again, he hoped he'd done the right thing.

But as he walked out of her house and back into the reality fate had given him one sunny day that had changed everything, he knew that he'd have to think about exactly what he wanted from Olivia— and for himself.

Because she was different, that much he knew. Putting her at arm's length for so long hadn't been wise for either of them, but maybe it had been what they needed. But now, maybe they needed more.

He didn't know, but he promised himself that by the next time he saw her, he'd know exactly what he wanted and he'd make sure that he never hurt her. He'd seen enough hurt in his lifetime, and he never wanted to be the cause of it for another.

Never again.

Chapter Five

Olivia knew she'd made a mistake, but she'd gotten used to making them. After all, she couldn't quite help herself when it came to Derek, and that was something she knew would have to change.

Was she going to meet him in a week? She didn't know, but part of her understood she wouldn't have a choice. Even if she didn't touch him, even if she didn't let herself break for him, she'd still have to tell him the truth. She should have done it already when he came by her house the week before, but she hadn't been thinking clearly. She'd been in shock at just seeing him again, at knowing that they had yet another connection she didn't know about, so much so that she'd lost the words she needed to say to him.

And that made her a horrible person.

She'd even been avoiding Austin and Sierra of late, telling herself that she needed to work and had hidden herself inside, ordering groceries and other things for the house so she didn't chance seeing them and somehow telling them everything she'd done. The connections were too clear now, the ties that bound them together fraying at the edges now that she knew that the Montgomerys were part of Derek's world.

Derek was going to hate her even more now, but there was nothing to be done about it. She'd made her bed, slept in it with Derek, and now she would have to lie in it until the end of her days, knowing what she'd done.

And because she knew she'd burst if she didn't let at least *something* out of her soon, she picked up her phone and called Alice.

Her friend and author was the one who usually called, with Olivia rarely making the calls herself, but desperate times called for desperate measures—and phone calls. As it was, whenever Alice called, Olivia was able to get whatever she needed to off her chest anyway. Alice knew her so well that the calls always came when they needed to. Today, however, she couldn't wait for her friend.

"What's wrong?" Alice didn't pull any punches and, apparently, the other woman knew something had to be up for Olivia to be the one to initiate the call.

"Nothing." Olivia let out a breath. "Okay, that was a total lie. I need to talk to someone about everything going on, but it's a long story, and I feel like I'm making something huge out of nothing or I'm not taking it seriously enough. I need help, Alice."

"Talk to me."

Alice lived across the country so it wasn't as if she could come over in a pinch and have a drink with Olivia like she might have wanted to if she had a core group of friends in town. Her business meant that she was constantly online and made friends that were true friends and closer to her than some of her friends in real life, though. But it also meant that having meet-ups that had nothing to do with work trips didn't really happen. Calling Alice from across the country was one of the only ways Olivia would be able to have a friend in her life for advice. That fact kind of saddened her, but that was the country they were living in now, and she would cope.

If she could figure out what to do about Derek, that was.

"Remember what I couldn't talk about before?"

"I do. Are you ready now?"

"I think I have to be. But if you're working—"

"I'm always working. Same as you. But I'm here for you. Talk, Olivia. What's wrong?"

And that was the thing about her friend. They both worked far too much for their own reasons, but Alice's husband supported the time she put into the career that was part of both of their lives. Olivia only had herself and her own timelines to worry about.

And that seemed to be enough for her. Or, at least, it had been.

"I met a man."

"Oh?"

"I...well, I met this man, Derek, four years ago." Olivia pinched the bridge of her nose. She still couldn't quite believe that it had been four years since she first saw the man who would change her life, even if she didn't realize it at the time.

"Derek? I like the name. Very hero worthy."

"You could say that. Only I didn't know his name was Derek until a little less than a month ago." She paused while Alice went silent. So quiet, and so unlike the other woman that Olivia was afraid she'd shocked her. "Alice?"

"I'm waiting for the rest. You just found out his name? Interesting. Now, tell me. Everything. Okay? Just let it all out, and I promise not to judge. But it sounds to me like you're going around the main issue because you're scared and you don't know what to do with the pieces you have. I'm your author. You're my editor. I'm usually the one who gives you the pieces while you help me arrange them. How about we switch it up for now?"

And this was why she'd called Alice. Her friend understood, even if Olivia didn't.

"I met Derek in a hotel bar four years ago. I'd been out on a blind date that ended ten minutes in when I found out he was married. The fact that it was a blind date at a four-star restaurant in a hotel seems a bit slimy now, but for some reason, I didn't think it was weird then. The woman that set me up—a friend who is no longer a friend—had thought the divorce was final. Not so much. So, I took myself to the bar after throwing my martini in the guy's face. I needed a second drink at that point and just wanted some peace to try and forget men and their horrible ways and just *be* before I headed home."

"Asshole."

"Indeed. I have no idea if the guy is still married or not, but it doesn't matter anyway. He's out of my life, and I hope his wife is okay because he really was an asshole. Where was I? Oh, yeah, so I was at the bar, and a man in dark jeans, a blue Henley, and a sexy beard comes up to me, taking the last seat at the bar. He was broad-shouldered, sexy as hell, and had a deep voice that went straight to the right places."

Alice gave a smoky laugh, and Olivia realized exactly how detailed she'd been just then. Apparently, Derek brought that out in her even when he wasn't near.

"We didn't speak for a few moments until he finally turned and smiled." She paused, remembering even as her heart ached. She loved that smile. Loved him if she were being honest. And she could never see him again. "I don't remember exactly what we said that first time. But we talked for over an hour and had more than a few drinks. He said he was visiting, though I didn't ask from where." She figured now that he'd most likely been at the hotel traveling for his job, but she really didn't know. She hadn't asked and was afraid she never would. Though now that she thought about it, there had been a tattoo convention near, so maybe he'd been staying for that and not just the shop?

"Somehow, we ended up in his hotel room."

"Damn, girl."

"I know. It was so unlike me. It's *still* so unlike me. And when we were through with each other, he said he wanted to see me again but couldn't until he came back to town. So we promised to meet again the next month. Same time. Same place. We made our promises to ourselves, no names, just sex, just time. And we kept with it for four years without missing a month. I can't believe we made it last as long as we did without finding out more about each other, but we did. And now...and now it's crazy."

"You called him Derek. So you must know his name now."

"He asked me to call him by his name this last time." She paused. "And that's how I realized I knew him."

Alice paused. "You know him? Of course you do. You've been sleeping with him for four years. I'm not judging. You know I wouldn't because what you're doing is damn hot and I know you're being careful because you wouldn't be Olivia if you weren't, so there must be something to it."

"I know him from when I was younger. Much younger. I didn't realize it was him because of the beard and, honestly, I never thought I'd see the Derek I knew again. He doesn't recognize me, though. I don't know why he would. It's been so long."

"And that means you can't see him again? Because, from the way you're sounding, I have a feeling you want to run away from him and what you could have."

Alice knew her far too well. "There are things...there are things I need to tell him before I tell anyone else. Reasons why I never should have been with him. Why I can't be with him again. I'll tell him. I have to. But I just don't know how."

Then she told Alice about the fact that Derek knew her neighbor and how he'd come over and that everything seemed to be falling apart around her. She was her own undoing, and she had to figure out the next step.

"Damn, girl. You have your work cut out for you. You sound like someone I'd write. And you know what the next page would be?"

"No, I'm the editor, not the author."

"You're the heroine, Olivia. Be heroic. Take a stand. Go to him on the day you're supposed to meet him and tell him what you need to. Maybe he'll be okay with whatever it is. Maybe he won't. But you owe it to yourself and possibly even him to make it right. Tell him. Take away that burden, and maybe you'll end up with the happiness I know you've always wanted."

Tears slid down Olivia's cheeks, and she quickly wiped them away. "I don't know what I'm going to do. I feel like there's so much on my chest, so much pressure, and yet it's not a huge thing in the grand scheme of things. It's not anything that's going to destroy someone's world." Only hers and perhaps Derek's. "I shouldn't be feeling like this. I shouldn't feel like everything's coming down on top of me."

"You're allowed to feel how you feel. Just because it's only part of your life and now Derek's, doesn't mean it's not important. If it affects you, then it's important. You're allowed to dwell. Now, go take a bath, read a book that has nothing to do with work, and think about what you're going to wear for your night. And, Olivia? I'll want more details when you're ready. I love you, babe. And I want to thank you for trusting me enough to tell me this part."

Olivia whispered her love and hung up, wondering what she was going to do next. She hated feeling out of sorts, hated wondering if she was making the right choices. She'd made the wrong choice years ago, and now she was having to face that once again.

Maybe she'd take that bath and let her mind wander to a book and not the man who crept into her dreams every night. Or maybe she'd dwell again and want to stay in the tub until it was ice-cold and her thoughts wrapped around her until she couldn't breathe.

With an annoyed sigh at the thoughts and feelings running through her, she went to her bathroom and started her bath. She'd pop on an audiobook and soak and maybe try to get her life together because she needed to make a choice, damn it. It was about time she came clean and told Derek that she knew him beyond their meeting four years ago and exactly how their paths had crossed. He'd hate her, but then again, she couldn't blame him.

By the time she had her glass of wine and her audiobook going, the tub was full, and she slid into the too-hot water, knowing it would cool quickly. She didn't have jets, but she could at least soak for an hour or two, and the tub was deep enough to cover her knees and boobs at the same time. It was the best bathtub she could have without going too expensive and fancy, and it was *hers*. It counted.

With her eyes closed, she tried to just be in the moment and listen to her book. Trying not to worry about what she needed to tell Derek and how that would all go down in the end, however, wasn't easy. But she tried.

So she let the hot water overheat her skin, let the romance novel on her speakers fill her thoughts, and when she got to an overly steamy part, she slid her hand out of the water, tried her best to dry it, and paused the audio book since she could only think about Derek and his very nice hands right then. He didn't deserve her thinking about him when she was feeling like this, achy and hot—not until he knew the truth. Yes, she'd made herself come countless times before while thinking of him, but that was when he'd been D, not Derek.

Her Derek.

No, he wasn't her Derek. He hadn't been before, and he never would be. And the sooner she got that through her head, the better.

With a sigh, she got out the tub, knowing it wasn't much use anymore. She'd just lie there thinking about what she couldn't change and feel like a damn idiot. So she let out the now cooling water, dried off, and grabbed her phone. It was getting late, so she might as well lie in bed and read a book since she usually had one on her tablet and one on her audio app all the time. She was a reader and couldn't help the fact that she constantly had books surrounding her.

And because she hadn't slept more than a couple of hours at a time for the past week, she fell asleep with her tablet on her chest and the lights still on. She hadn't even done her nightly routine, but sleep had taken over.

As did the nightmares.

She had them from time to time and knew she'd never be able to stop them. They always hit her full force when they did come. Sometimes, she was back in the body of her younger self, watching the world shift on its axis without her being able to change her actions. Other times, she was herself as an adult, watching two young girls play in the sunlight, laughing and smiling. Then the shadows would come, and there would be no more laughter, no more smiles.

Only screams.

Only agony.

Only nothingness.

Like the other times she'd had those nightmares, Olivia sat straight up in bed, her body drenched in sweat, tablet crashing to the floor, and the scream tearing from her throat loud enough that anyone near her who was still awake would have been able to hear it.

But there was no one near.

There never was.

Because she was alone. Just like she had to be. Just like she always would be.

And next week when she saw Derek again, she would tell him about her dreams and explain it all. He deserved to know the truth, deserved to know that the woman he'd held in his arms for all this time wasn't who he thought she was.

After all, he wasn't who she'd thought he was either.

He was so much more…and that meant it would have to be the end.

Inevitably.

Chapter Six

Just a little more ink, a little more care, and Derek would be done for the day. At least that's what he told himself after a long-ass day that never seemed to end. He might love his job, but today, he wanted nothing more than to go home and beat the shit out of something so he could let all the raw energy he had swirling inside out.

Tomorrow, he'd see Olivia.

If she showed up.

And he couldn't think of anything else.

Damn it.

And even though he wanted to see her because he wanted her, he knew it was more than that. He wanted to know more about her, wanted to see if maybe he'd take that chance and see if she could be part of his life. She lived so damn close to him. At first, he'd thought maybe she lived out of town like he did, but now that he knew they lived close to one another and had a few of the same friends, he thought maybe that had to mean something.

He'd spent most of his life trying to help others through their issues, but now he had to work through his own. Because most of that time helping others meant helping his mom. She hadn't been the same since his sister Stacey died. Hell, *he* hadn't been the same and wasn't sure any of them ever could be again. But his mom had broken completely.

And while he hadn't been able to piece her back together, he'd tried his hardest, no matter the cost. Then, he'd helped his friends around the shop navigate their relationships as if he had any clue how to connect with another person that way. Before Olivia, he'd had short-lived relationships with women over time, but never anything concrete. He'd never let himself get to that point. He had to be there for his mom and, hell, if he were honest, he'd never wanted to open himself to someone where he might end up losing more of himself in the process. He'd done that before he was old enough to understand what love was, and he hadn't planned to ever do it again.

But Olivia? Something about her called to him.

Hell, he'd been lying to himself for four years if he ever really thought that going to her one night a month was just because they were good in bed together. Something about her drew him in, and he wanted to know more about what that was. He'd stayed away from anything else that could hurt him for so long, he was afraid he'd missed out on something that was truly important.

He just hoped that she didn't run away again like the last time.

Or that she showed up at all.

Yeah, he knew where she lived and could get her contact information quickly, but he wouldn't. That wasn't their agreement, and he'd already reneged on it once before by going to Austin's house. He wasn't going to turn into that creepy stalker that forced himself into her presence. If she wanted him, she'd ask, and he'd be there.

If not?

Well, then, that would fucking suck, and he'd have to figure out what to do about it.

He needed to get out of his head and back onto his work. His client was waiting for him out at his station, and Derek had been standing alone in the back office holding his sketch pad for like ten minutes. If he wasn't careful, he would fuck up a tattoo, and that wasn't something he did. Ever.

Hell, that wasn't something that was allowed in Montgomery Ink.

Austin would beat the shit out of him.

Then Maya would fillet his skin right off.

Okay, so the two of them wouldn't actually get violent, but getting yelled at, or worse, fired because he had his mind on Olivia and not his job wasn't something he was keen on trying.

Even as he made his way out of the office, Austin was there with one brow raised and his mouth set in a firm line under that big-ass beard of his.

"You okay?" his boss asked, his arms folded over his chest as he leaned against the wall nearest the office. On the other side of the wall was where they had the private room for piercings and clients who wanted privacy. Maya was in there with a client getting a full thigh piece at the moment, so Derek was glad it was Austin who was in front of him and not her.

He, like any sane individual, was a little scared of Maya Montgomery-Gallagher.

"I'm fine. Just needed to clear my head. Jason still waiting on me?"

Austin nodded. "The guy has his book out and is zoning. You don't usually take long breaks like some of us need to for our aging backs, so what's really happening inside that head of yours?"

Derek shook his head. "Let me finish up on Jason first."

"Then you'll tell me exactly what's wrong? Because we don't like seeing you like this. I didn't ask what happened when you went over to Olivia's, and I'm still feeling a little like I crossed a line. She's our friend, too, and from what I've seen, she doesn't have a whole lot of those around her."

Derek muttered a curse but nodded. "Yeah, I get that. And I don't know what's going on with us, but I'm hopefully seeing her tomorrow."

Austin's eyes narrowed. "It's been a month, then?"

"I just hope to hell she shows up."

Austin reached out and gripped Derek's shoulder, giving it a tight squeeze. "If it's meant to be, she will. She's quiet sometimes but has a great sense of humor and wit. Just like you. I can see the two of you together, so I hope it works out. Just don't fucking hurt her, okay? Because it's not going to be Maya or even me who kicks your ass if you do."

Derek winced. "Sierra?"

"My wife has been trying to get Olivia to join the Montgomery girls' club for over a year now, and I'm pretty sure she's not going to take no for an answer again. And once Olivia is part of the core group? Well then, you've got the whole lot of them on your tail. And Sierra can take a man down if she has to. Believe me."

Derek let out a sigh, nodding. "Understood. I don't want to hurt Olivia."

"Then make sure you know exactly what you want when you see her again. Because she deserves that. Got me?"

"I get you," he mumbled, then shouldered past so he could focus on his job and not his love life. Love life? Hell, did he love her? No, he didn't think he could, not when he didn't know enough about her to form that kind of opinion. But he liked her. A lot. And not just because of how they were together in bed. He wanted to know more about her, more about what they could be.

And maybe that was an answer in itself.

He didn't want to be the one fleeing, and that meant he sure as hell hoped she didn't want to run away either.

By the time he got home, he was still on edge, but at least he didn't need to head down to the basement for his punching bag. He'd gotten a lot of stress out of his system by just doing his job and making sure the final product on Jason's skin was flawless. That had been their third session on the full right shoulder and sleeve, and while they might have to meet up in another month to make sure they had every angle perfect once the swelling went down, he and Jason were both happy with the results.

Of course, thinking about meeting up with Jason after a month only made him think about seeing Olivia tomorrow, and the next month, and the one after that. Only Derek didn't think he'd be able to wait a month between visits anymore. He wanted to know her, wanted her in his life, and that meant he needed to see her for more than a few hours when the moon was high in the sky.

It would be a big change going from what they had to what he wanted, but that was what happened in relationships. Things progressed. Theirs hadn't for so long because they'd made sure they had their rules. But what if their so-called rules had been shit to begin with? It seemed to him that they'd only implemented them to keep each other at a distance, and not just for the fun they thought they had.

He knew why he kept her at a distance, and it had to do with protecting himself. But why did she keep him at arm's length? And what did she need to tell him? She'd been so damn cryptic and seemingly worried, and because he was an asshole and had kissed her instead of listening, he hadn't been able to hear what she had to say. It was his fault, he knew, but he would hear her out, would listen like he should have—tomorrow night.

Derek let out a groan just thinking about her, and all that excess energy came rushing back in a hard wave. But instead of anger, it went straight to his cock, and he knew if he didn't get some release, he'd feel as if he were going to burst.

Since he was alone and didn't have any other plans except to sit and wallow over Olivia, he lifted his ass off the couch, undid his jeans to slide them down a bit, and fisted the base of his cock.

He shifted slightly so he could get a better hold, then slowly slid his hand up and down his length. Since he didn't have any lotion or lube near, he spit into his hand to help him glide easier, then rested his head back on the couch, slowly and methodically running his hand over his dick. He let himself imagine Olivia doing the same to him, her eyes on him, wide and dark as she took him in hand, being gentle at first before squeezing hard and fondling his balls. At that thought, he picked up the pace, imagining himself fucking her tits, then leaning back as she licked and sucked down his cock. She was so damn good with her hands and her tongue. Usually, he was the one who took control in bed, even when she went down on him, but sometimes, she was the one with all the control, and if he was honest with himself, even with him leading her, she was always the one with the power.

And he damn well liked that.

With that thought and the idea of him sinking into her wet heat in mind, he came into his hand with a wet rush and did his best to come on his shirt rather than around his living room like a heathen. Thankfully, he had decent aim, even when he was losing himself in thoughts of Olivia.

As reality began to sink in, he rolled up his shirt a bit and then stripped it off from behind, doing his best not to spread his mess around. He was alone in his house, masturbating on his couch to the thoughts of a woman he wanted in his life while he was pretty sure she wanted to run again.

He'd officially hit another version of his rock bottom.

By the time he'd put his shirt in the washer along with his jeans and the rest of his clothes from the hamper and washed up, he was annoyed with himself. He put on some gym shorts, not bothering with underwear since he wasn't planning to go anywhere, and walked into the kitchen for a beer. That's when the phone in his pocket buzzed that familiar tone once again, and he gritted his teeth, knowing this call wouldn't be good. None of them had been recently, but there was nothing he could do about it except listen and try to be a good son.

His mom had always loved Stacey more than she did him. It was a fact he'd never gotten out of his head, but he'd learned to live with it long ago.

"Mom."

"I hate myself."

Jesus. He hated himself too because all he wanted to do was hang up and try to get her to go and get help again. Only she wouldn't, and he was all she had left, so he'd never do that to her, even if it took a little sliver of his soul with each passing day and every call she made.

But she was his mother, and he was going to do his best by her, even if it wasn't enough.

Was it any wonder that he wanted to shield himself from anyone else that could get too close for too long? He already had enough on his plate as it was.

"Mom." He tried to keep his voice patient. He was always so patient with her. He loved his mother and would continue to until the end of his days and perhaps even beyond that, but she took every ounce of his energy at times.

She deserved so much more, though, and that was something he needed to remember.

She'd been through hell and had clawed her way back out, bloody and broken, only to be kicked again when Dad left.

Derek was all she had left, and yet he felt as if he wasn't enough. He couldn't blame himself for it, though; she'd tried hard for too long and now she just was who she was, a shadow of her former self, with hardly a resemblance to the woman who used to cut up his and

Stacey's sandwiches into little hearts and other shapes for school then eat the leftover pieces herself since she hated wasting food.

"Derek. I'm tired."

He leaned against the counter, giving himself a moment before he went to put on clothes and grab his keys. He always went to her when she needed him, and every time around a holiday, anniversary, or birthday, she got worse. They were a couple of months away from a trigger, but she was still having a bad day. It was obvious. He hated this for her and knew that no matter how much help he tried to get her, how much help he tried to *give* her, it might not ever be enough.

"I know, Mom. I know. What can I do?"

"Nothing. There's nothing anyone can do. I hate this, Derek. Why can't everything go back to how I need it to? Why did it all have to change?"

"I'm sorry, Mom. There's nothing I can say to make it better. Nothing I can say ever makes it better. But I'm here. And if you need me, I'll sit with you right now."

She let out a long sigh that went straight to his heart. "I'm sorry for calling. I don't need you. I just need my family back."

He was her family, too, but he didn't say that. Instead, he listened in silence for a few more moments before she hung up on him, then he took his phone to his room and changed into a pair of jeans and a clean shirt. He quickly stuffed his clothes from the washer into the dryer since he'd used the quick cycle and then grabbed his keys and headed to his car.

He'd go sit with his mom and just listen. She more than likely wouldn't have anything to say to him, but then again, she rarely did. But he'd be there for her as he always was. He hated that she was constantly in pain about things that were out of both his and her control, but he'd try to help her now.

He hadn't been able to protect his sister when it mattered most. He hadn't been enough for his father when times had gotten too rough and leaving had seemed the easier choice. So Derek would be damned if he gave up on his mother when she was at her worst.

And even as he slid into his car and headed down the familiar roads to his mother's house, a different one than the one he'd grown up in since that had been too much for everyone, Olivia's face flashed through his mind.

Tomorrow was supposed to be their night. That was when he was going to take a risk. And yet it seemed so much harder when his past kept coming back and hitting him hard in the face with each phone call from his mother.

Life was never easy, but living after the dead had moved on and you hadn't was harder than he'd ever thought possible.

Chapter Seven

A week had passed, and Olivia couldn't catch her breath. Why had she waited until the hotel to see him again? She should have been the adult and gone over to Austin and Sierra's and asked for Derek's number. It would have been better for everyone if she'd been able to tell Derek what she needed to without being in a place with so many shared memories between them. Now, she'd either have to make a public scene in the hotel bar or risk going up to the room that he no doubt had already arranged. It would likely be a different room than all the others before, but it would still feel like *theirs*. It didn't matter if the bed had been updated, if the view from the window was different, or if they'd found themselves on each floor over the years. It would still be their room. And once the door closed behind her, she'd have to tell him who she was so he'd know the truth.

A small part of her hoped that he'd understand. That he'd know that she hadn't kept it from him for years, only the past month as she pieced herself together once she figured out who he was. A small part of her held the dreams where he would say he understood and still kiss her. Still want her. That he'd forgive her for what had happened all those years ago and they would be able to *be* again.

But that piece was a liar. She *knew* that. Because no matter how nice the hotel was, no matter the leather seats and ornate molding, she didn't fit here. Neither did he. They had been playing a part all these years, a role that had been a lie—even if she hadn't understood it at the time. Because their rules had meant nothing in the end. She'd still ended up falling, still ended up making connections. And she had no idea what to do about it. Or rather, she knew what she *should* do even if it would hurt her more than she thought possible.

She didn't want to lose him.

Yet, she'd never really had him.

She'd made the choice to show up at the hotel, made a decision to dress like she normally did for their encounters, so she could have some form of armor for what she needed to tell him. And yet, some part of her knew that if Derek kissed her first, she might go weak and let him love her one last time before she lost it all.

He deserved far more than that, but she knew tonight would be their last time.

She was going to go to hell paved with those good intentions, and once again, she had to fight for breath.

She wore a deep purple dress that hugged her torso, tucked in around her waist and flared out at her thighs. It had layers and swaths to hug her curves while being flowy at the same time. She loved this dress but knew she might not wear it again if Derek were to push her out of his life forever.

Once she told him who she was now that she truly knew, there would be no happily ever after for her. There would be no talking it over and trying to remember the good times.

There would be no more D and O.

She held back a smile, thinking of the little jokes they'd made at the fact that he was D and she was O. It might have been immature, but they'd both laughed, both smiled, then had both fallen back into bed together.

They'd done that often.

"Is this seat taken?"

She closed her eyes at the sound of his deep voice. She didn't turn, wasn't sure she could face him, but then she reminded herself that tonight wasn't about her. It was about Derek and what she needed to tell him.

So she sucked in a deep breath, ignored the tightening in her belly, and turned on her stool to face him. She lifted her chin, gesturing for him to sit down. She wasn't sure she could formulate the words just then. She would, though. The martini near her elbow remained untouched, and as he took the seat next to her, she licked her lips.

His gaze went to the action, and she could have cursed herself for doing that. She couldn't lead him on, but neither could she stop her physical responses when it came to being in Derek's presence.

"That's a new dress. I like it."

He must have looked at her as he walked up to the bar because his eyes were only on hers now. She loved the way his eyes locked on hers, the way she could tell so much about him just from the way he looked at her. She knew those eyes, knew them as the man he was, and now that she focused, she could see the fragments of memories from when he was the boy who had gotten annoyed when she followed him around because she'd fallen in love with her best friend's older brother. Of course, she hadn't been old enough to actually love him beyond a childhood crush.

No, those feelings came later.

She swallowed hard. She couldn't love him. Not now, not later. She didn't know him, not enough for those feelings to make sense. At least that's what she kept reminding herself.

"Olivia. Are you okay?"

She pulled herself out of her thoughts and tried to make it look as if she weren't going in a thousand different directions inside herself.

"It's not a new dress."

He frowned. "Oh. I guess I don't know all of your dresses. I've seen a few." He paused. "Touched a few, but I guess I don't know them all."

She closed her eyes, taking a deep breath through her nose. "Sorry. I'm being weird."

"No, you aren't. I called you Olivia. I didn't even bother with O or trying to do what we normally do and act as if we don't know each other. It's different. And it should be. This isn't like the last time or any of the other times before that. And maybe that's okay. Hell, after all this time, it feels new *because* it's already different. And, yeah, I don't know every dress you've ever owned, and you don't know everything about me either, but we can see if we want to try."

Olivia looked down and played with the rim of her martini glass, not sure what she was going to say because her heart was in her throat at that moment. He wanted more? Or at least wanted to see if they had more? Though he'd alluded to something like that before when he was in her home, she hadn't really put any weight to it. And since she felt as if she were about to black out whenever he was near her, she didn't really remember anything he'd said.

"We should talk," she said softly, trying to make herself sound as if she weren't panicking inside. From the way he looked at her, she wasn't sure she'd succeeded.

He tilted his head, studied her, then reached out to brush her hair back from her shoulders. She hadn't bothered with the pins today since it would have been a temptation for her that she had wanted to try to resist. She'd thought about it once she looked in the mirror and imagined his hands in her hair like he'd done so many times over the years. So she'd left it down, leaving the temptation behind. Only when he moved her hair, his fingertips brushed the skin of her shoulder over the straps of her dress, and she sucked in a breath. His eyes darkened, and she knew he felt it, too—that need, that yearning.

And she hated herself just a little bit for it because she was going to change everything.

She had to.

"We should. Do you want to talk down here? Or up in the room?"

Anywhere but the room.

She didn't say that, of course, since the only answer *was* the room, but it didn't make her words come out any easier.

"I don't really want to talk down here," she answered finally and slid off the stool.

"Do you want to finish your drink?" he asked, then raised a brow. "Or maybe start it?"

She shook her head. "I don't think I can drink anything right now, and I only got it so I wasn't sitting at the bar without holding something. You know?"

"I do. Though I wish I'd gotten here earlier so you weren't here alone in that case."

She shrugged and picked up her bag. "I'm always early to everything. I can't help it."

"Good to know. See? We're already learning new things."

Oh, if he only knew.

He took her hand, and she did her best not to pull away, not because she didn't want his touch, but because she wanted it too much. And just like the previous times he'd led her to the elevator, she wondered what people thought as they looked at the two of them. Did they think they were lovers? A couple? Or were they having an illicit affair?

As none of those were the truth, she couldn't help but wonder what those who had noticed them over time would think when Olivia and Derek didn't show up again.

Would they worry?

Would they think it was over?

Or would their absence go unnoticed, a bare blip of a memory that didn't mean anything to the casual observer?

She didn't want to be a memory long faded, but as she only had the memories of what had once been swirling in her mind, she wasn't sure she could be anything else and remain sane.

"Why do you look so scared?" Derek asked as he pressed the button for the seventh floor on the elevator.

Lucky number seven? Or to the seventh layer of hell in Dante's Inferno?

"I'm fine."

"You think I don't know you, but I do know enough to know that's a lie. Let's get into the room so you can finally tell me what's got you so on edge. Hmm?"

She didn't answer, but as they walked to the room once they left the elevator, her silence was answer enough. He pressed his keycard to the sensor and opened the door, gesturing for her to go in first. She hated that her chest hurt, that her lungs felt as if they were too large for her ribcage.

She had to do this quickly, like ripping off a Band-Aid, and then she'd be fine.

And if she kept telling herself that, maybe she'd actually believe it.

The door closed behind them, and she rolled her shoulders back. Time to be the woman she'd fought so hard to be and tell him the truth. So she turned on her heel to face him...and found his lips on hers.

Damn this man and his mouth.

Damn him.

Her lips parted without her knowing, and he deepened the kiss, his hands going in her hair and over her face, pulling her in closer. He tasted of mint and a little bit of coffee, and she wanted to drown in his essence forever. But even as she thought that, even as he groaned, she knew she needed to pull away.

And unlike the last time, she did.

"Stop, Derek. I need to talk to you."

He panted just as she did, but took a step back. The heat of him still touched her, but his body didn't, and for that she was grateful.

Kissing him again would be wrong. Falling for him would be even worse.

She'd already done both, but she'd be damned if she let herself fall into bed with him again. She couldn't hold back this secret from him and let him touch her, let him *take* her. She'd never forgive herself.

"What's wrong, Olivia? What's so bad that you look as if you want to cry and shake at the same time? I know I've been pushing you, and for that, I'm sorry. If you want to go back to what we had before, we can. We can do our thing once a month and keep each other at just first names and never talk again outside of that. But you need to know I want more. I *need* more. But I'll settle for what we had if that's all you have to give. However, if you can give me more? I'll take it. I want to know you. I want to see you outside these walls. I want to go on actual dates with you and find out who we can be together when we're not playing by the rules we set when we didn't know any better. And I know I'm saying all the things I want, but hell, we've done so good for so long by not saying anything too deep, not letting each other get too close to who we are, that maybe it's time we break that mold. Maybe it's time we actually say what we want, rather than what we think we need."

She was breaking inside, large chasms ripping through her body as if a quake set off a chain reaction of pain and despair. Yet she could be strong for him, strong now when she hadn't been before.

He wanted more. She'd known that, of course, but hearing him say the words, seeing the plea in his eyes, she couldn't catch her breath.

She wanted all of that, too. Wanted that and more, but she couldn't even let herself think it until she told him what she'd been holding back.

"My name's Olivia," she blurted.

He frowned, clearly caught off guard by her saying something he already knew.

"Yes, you told me that last time. What's wrong?"

"My name's Olivia Madison. Does that name sound familiar?"

He froze, his face going blank.

He remembered.

But she needed to tell him everything, just in case. Yes, it would be more for her at this point, but it could be for him, too.

"I was three years old when I found my best friend. She was the same age as me, and her big brother was only a year or two older than us. She was everything to me. Her light blond hair was the opposite of mine, her pale skin so much lighter than mine, and I loved that we were so different on the outside, yet so much the same on the inside. I didn't know what all of that meant when I was a little girl, but I know now. She was my everything, my best friend for the next three years of my life."

He didn't say anything, but he clenched his jaw as well as his fists.

He knew.

He remembered.

But she wasn't done yet.

"Stacey and I used to play out in the big field behind our homes. We were next-door neighbors, but our yards weren't all that big and didn't have enough room for us to play. So we used the field with all the grass and hills and flowers. Our parents let us, knowing we'd be safe because they could see us from the top-floor windows of our houses as long as they looked out. We should have been safe."

Derek kept his silence, and she wanted to throw up, but she kept going. If she stopped now, she'd hate herself.

"One day, we were chasing butterflies. We were six, and that's how we worked; we needed them for our princess court. You see, the butterflies would be our ladies in waiting, and we would be dual princesses in our kingdom. Stacey was the one with the imagination; I was the one who helped add the little details like butterflies to make sure it all made sense."

Even then, she'd been her best friend's editor in their own little world.

But even then, she hadn't been enough.

Olivia took a deep breath and continued. "That day, though, we got too close to the road. I don't know how, but we ended up right on the curve. I called out to Stacey, telling her to be careful, but she turned at the wrong time at the sound of my voice. She didn't see the curb."

She let out a shuddering breath, and her eyes stung, but she didn't let any tears fall. Stacey might have deserved them, but Olivia didn't.

"She took one too many steps right at the worst moment. No one saw the car coming. The driver didn't see her."

"I remember," he growled out. "You don't have to go into any more details. I remember my fucking sister, Olivia. Question is, how long have you known? How long did you know I was that boy? How long have you lied to me, keeping this from me?"

This time, the tears fell. "I only knew when you said your name and I put it all together. I promise you. You and your family moved away right after everything happened, and I haven't seen you since I was six. I never thought I would see you again. I never thought that you, D, could possibly be the Derek I knew as a little girl and had a crush on."

She hadn't meant to say that last part, but she was baring the rest of herself so she might as well keep going.

"I don't know if I can believe you."

That hurt, but then again, she didn't blame him. She'd already broken more than once in her life, and now it was her turn to break him so he could do the same to her once more.

"I'm so sorry, Derek. I didn't mean to call out right at that moment and distract her. I didn't mean for any of that to happen. I will never forgive myself for that day, and I will never forgive myself for making you think I ever wanted to hurt you. I didn't know who you were until that moment last month when I pulled away, but I don't know how I can get you to believe me. I've tried to find the courage and the words to tell you since then. I don't know what else to say except that I'm so sorry. I'm so sorry that we lost Stacey. I'm sorry that I'm that girl from all those years ago who brings with her those bad memories, and that you're that same boy. And I'm sorry that I fell for you when I shouldn't have. I broke the rules. I changed everything. And I'm just so damn sorry."

She'd torn herself open, laid herself bare in every way she could, and now there was nothing else for her.

She just prayed that she'd be enough, that the small part of her that had once held hope would shine.

But, of course, it didn't.

It wouldn't.

Derek gave her one last look, opened his mouth to say something, then stopped. When he turned on his heel and walked out of the hotel room, she knew it would be for the last time. This would be their last month.

He was gone.

And she knew that no matter what some small part of her had thought and hoped, she deserved nothing less.

Only when the door slammed closed did she fall to her knees, ignoring the way her dress rode up and wrinkled, to let her tears fall freely.

She'd broken once more, but this time, she wasn't sure she'd be able to find the pieces to put herself back together.

She'd given in to that hope, even if she hadn't wanted to. She'd fallen for the man she promised herself she'd never fall for.

Her rules were clear: never fall in love.

But she had.

Never commit.

But she'd thought she could.

And never tell Derek the truth.

But she had.

And now, it was over.

Forever.

Chapter Eight

Shock was a funny thing. Made a person do some of the worst things possible without feeling a damn thing. Derek hadn't been able to feel a single part of his body once Olivia started talking. He'd gone numb and then had stood there like an idiot, trying to understand what exactly she was trying to tell him and how it all fit into the orderly life and memories he'd built over the years.

The O from his bed, the one who had been in his dreams for the past four years, was the same Olivia who had been there the day his family had broken apart—who had been there countless times before that.

He still couldn't quite believe it.

Derek ran his hands through his hair and tried to steady his breathing. The part of him that had fallen for Olivia over the last four years knew he shouldn't have left her standing in the hotel room like that, looking as if she'd broken right along with him. But the other part of him hadn't been able to look at her and not remember everything he'd lost.

He hadn't been able to separate the two parts of himself as he tried to digest the information and whatever he felt about the words coming from her mouth.

He had no idea what he should have done or even what he was supposed to do now. Somehow, he'd driven himself home, leaving Olivia behind like the right asshole he was, and all so he could think.

But now that he was in his house, on his couch, he couldn't think of a damn thing.

Olivia had been the little girl who ran around with Stacey every day as if they had no cares in the world. They'd been so young, so free-spirited, that yeah, they *hadn't* had any true cares to weigh them down. They were little girls, they shouldn't have had to deal with the big issues anyway.

Now that he really thought about it, he could see some of the same hints of the girl he'd known in the woman he found years later. The shape of her eyes, the corners of her smile. But the younger Olivia had always smiled brighter, always had such an innocence about her that shone in her eyes. A purity she'd been allowed to have because she was way too young to deal with any of the crap that had come after Stacey's accident. Hell, he'd had the same innocence, at least he liked to think he did. Then, everything changed, and he honestly hadn't thought of Olivia again.

Maybe he should have.

"Jesus Christ," he muttered to himself, annoyed that he'd let himself get this twisted. Not over a woman, but over a past he couldn't change.

He *knew* it hadn't been Olivia's fault. Hell, Stacey had run out into the road on her own before that day and likely would have anyway without Olivia calling out to her. The driver of the car had said as much, and while he hadn't spoken to the man in over a decade, he knew that he had never forgiven himself.

It seemed that no one had forgiven themselves in the past decades with regards to the tragedy.

The driver sure hadn't, but he also hadn't contacted Derek or his family to try to apologize or talk things out, at least not since the random phone call he'd placed when Derek was a teenager. It was after Derek's father had left, and when his mother had been going down one of her spirals. The driver had even said that it would be the last time he would call, but he wanted to let Derek and his family know that he'd always be thinking of Stacey. Derek hadn't known how he felt about it at the time, but over the years as Derek learned a bit more about who he was and how he dealt with his own grief, he knew that whatever the driver needed to do in order to live with what happened, Derek understood.

It hadn't been the driver's fault. It was an accident. And though Derek's mother had accused the driver at first, she'd really blamed herself—and even Derek—for the accident. She'd blamed God and fate and everyone she could. But none of that guilt had been able to bring Stacey back. None of that had been able to bring his mother back.

His father had blamed Derek for not watching Stacey, even though Derek had only been a year older and far too young to be responsible. That didn't stop his dad from being the asshole he was. The man had dealt with his grief by taking his rage out on Derek. Never with his fists, but words hurt enough. Then, his father hadn't been able to deal with Derek's mother's grief and breakdowns, so he'd just left one night without a word and hadn't looked back. There'd been money for child support until Derek turned eighteen, along with divorce papers, but for all intents and purposes, when Derek lost his sister, he'd lost his father and mother, as well.

Mom had checked out mentally, Dad emotionally, and Derek had been left to pick up the pieces.

Yet it had taken Derek far too long to find the pieces to pick up, and then he realized he didn't have enough to make up who he once thought he was.

But through all of that, he'd never once blamed the little girl who was with his sister that fateful day. Maybe he should have thought of Olivia more, but he'd only been seven years old and had just lost his little sister. He lived in a warzone within the confines of his home, and then he'd been pulled out of the only place he'd ever known and moved to a new one as soon as his mother was able.

I never blamed her, he repeated to himself.

And now that he could breathe, now that he could think, he knew she probably blamed herself far more than he would ever think to. He didn't even blame her for not telling him right away. If what she'd said was true, and hell, he believed her, then she hadn't known until he'd said his name.

He'd known once he told her to call him Derek that things would change, he just hadn't realized the how or the extent of it. And they *had* changed. He'd thought at first it was because he'd asked too much of her but, apparently, it had been the trigger for her to remember who he was from all those years ago.

No wonder she'd wanted to leave and never see him again.

He was the visual memory of that pain in her life.

The thing was, she was the same for him.

Now he wasn't sure he'd ever be able to look at her and not think of Stacey and that day with the butterflies.

That was the problem. He might not blame Olivia for what happened, but just her face would now make him remember that pain day in and day out. Was he strong enough to get through that? He didn't know, but that was something he needed to think about before he made any decisions. And no matter what happened in the hotel room earlier, he hadn't actually made the decision.

He didn't know what he was going to do about Olivia, but he knew he needed to do something…before he lost her and perhaps himself forever.

And before he could think himself into a headache, his phone buzzed, and he groaned. It was like the woman knew exactly when to call in order to make Derek hate himself even more.

He answered on the third ring. "Mom."

"I want to make cookies, but I'm out of peanut butter. Can you pick some up?"

It was seven at night, and the woman wanted to make cookies. Didn't even think about if Derek might be working or if he had plans. But that was his mother now, and there was nothing he could do about it or he'd risk losing her forever.

"I bought you some last week," Derek said. "And it's late, Mom. You should be relaxing before bed." It wasn't late, but it felt like it for his mother.

"I'm the mother. You're the son. You don't get to tell me what to do."

Jesus. "I know, Mom. But it's late. Get ready for bed and we can make cookies tomorrow if you want."

"Never mind, I don't want to make cookies now."

Then she hung up, and Derek looked at his phone, wondering how exactly he was going to deal with his mother for the rest of his life. It wasn't always this bad. He could go weeks without hearing from her because she'd ingrained herself into society and a healthy life. But, sometimes, it was like how it had been this past month.

He'd never tell his mother about Olivia. Ever.

Olivia didn't need that in her life.

And that was just one more reason it might be good for him to never see Olivia again. The thing was, though, he *wanted* to see her again. Wanted her in his life. He just wasn't sure if he could handle the cost or what that cost might even be after he thought more about it.

His mother would always be a part of his life. He was the only one left for her, and she was still his mom no matter what had happened in the past. That meant if he had Olivia in his life, as well, there would always be that tension. It would be something they'd either work through or not be strong enough for.

Olivia was already so damn strong, and now he was afraid that he'd be the weak one.

He'd once again thought himself into a corner, and knew that if he didn't just breathe and maybe have a beer so he could relax, he'd end up with an ulcer and still no decisions.

Memories of every time he'd had Olivia in his arms and how he felt when he wanted her to know his name came back to him. He'd wanted her as part of his life. He'd wanted *more*. He'd gone tonight knowing that she might not be there but hoping she would be. He'd gone to ask her to be in his life and to be more than just a single night a month. He'd broken all the rules and had laid himself bare for her.

And though he hadn't known every part of her—clearly—he'd known enough. The woman who had stood in front of him had been broken more than once, had shaken when she told him the truth. But she had told him. Had known that everything could and would change when she did so. He could never fault her for that.

And the thing was, he'd fallen for her. He fucking loved her and wanted more from her, wanted to give more of himself to her in the process. He just hoped that he'd be able to not think of Stacey when it came to Olivia.

So he would sit, and he would wait. He would think, and he would talk it out with himself until it all made sense. And if it never became clear, then he'd know his answer.

Because he hadn't fallen for the idea of Olivia, he'd fallen for more. They knew more about each other than they'd planned because there had been no way *not* to learn more with four years' worth of meetings. He knew the kind of woman she was, and knew that if he could find the strength to remember what they could have rather than what he'd lost, what *they'd* lost, they could be something great.

He just needed to get over himself and make that happen.

At least, he hoped.

Chapter Nine

Olivia had known the night before could've gone worse, but she wasn't sure how. Well, Derek could have thrown something, could have yelled, could have done a lot more than he did. But that wasn't him. He'd asked the questions he needed to, the ones that had come to him in the moment, then he'd left without a word, leaving her alone in the hotel room where any other time they would have shared each other's bodies and learned little snippets of who they were.

Because she knew she'd been lying to herself when she thought she hadn't given him a part of herself along the way. She might not have known every detail, but she knew the heart of him and knew she'd been transparent enough for him to learn the heart of her.

They'd known each other despite the rules.

She'd fallen for him against her subconscious wishes and surely against his, as well.

And he'd left. But it wasn't as if she could blame him. She'd gone through what felt like her entire life learning not to blame herself—at least not entirely—for what had happened with Stacey, but seeing Derek again, knowing who he was, had forced her to revert back to the young girl who only blamed herself.

She'd had therapy, she'd talked through her feelings until she was a wrung-out shell learning to fill herself back up with a new version of who she could and should be. But one breath, one look at Derek, and she was back to the girl with daisy chains on her head, chasing butterflies with her best friend. Then, the next breath, she was no longer the woman who had found her strength, but the younger woman, the child, who couldn't sleep without screaming.

Olivia let out a breath before running her hand through her hair, undoing the clip in the back. Then, she shook her hair out before twisting it back up so it lay in spirals around her head. She hadn't bothered to blow it out after the shower, so now it was in partial waves and curls with a few straight parts to round out the bunch. Hence why she tried not to wash her hair as much as possible.

And if she thought about her hair and cleaning habits, she wouldn't think about Derek, Stacey, or any work she needed to do. Because heartbreak wasn't an actual excuse to miss her deadlines. Her authors were counting on her, so it wasn't as if she could put her emptiness into an email and make them understand.

Her authors wrote romance.

But Olivia didn't live it.

Clearly.

She'd known she wouldn't be enough, but that was okay, that was her lot in life, and she'd move on eventually. She'd find something else to do on those nights she'd always looked forward to. Once she could stand straight again without wanting to break down, she'd roll her shoulders back and perhaps leave the house for longer than it took to get her delivery from her porch.

She'd be the Olivia who she needed to be again because that was the only answer for her.

She just needed to not feel as if she were dying inside first.

"One step at a time," she whispered to herself, then opened her laptop. She had a final read-through to complete and couldn't do that if she hadn't even opened the file.

Thankfully, her phone buzzed at that exact instant, so she didn't have to bother trying to see the screen through tear-filled eyes.

"Alice." Her voice didn't crack, so she counted that as a win. She ignored the fact that it sounded hollow, however. Alice would be able to tell her mood well enough from the lack of emotion anyway.

"Do I need to fly there? Because you sound like I need to fly there. I have the miles. We'll sit and drink and work because we're workaholics and know nothing else, but I'll be right by your side."

At that, Olivia broke down into tears, great hiccupping sobs that she knew she'd feel later once the numbness lifted from her chest. She'd texted Alice the night before, telling her friend that Derek had left. She hadn't wanted Alice to worry but hadn't been able to find the words to say anything else.

Olivia's body shook, and she swallowed hard, trying to catch her breath, but the tears felt good even as they ripped at the part of her she'd been trying to hide, the part that was raw and aching and just wanted to be loved. She'd always hated that part of herself, had felt as if it were weak. But she was wrong.

She was stronger with it, and now she wasn't sure what would happen to that layer when she escaped from the ashes of this moment.

"You better, baby?" Alice asked, her voice soft. "Get it out. Cry all you want, all you need to, and I'll be here. I'll be there, too. If you need me. Just say the word. I won't rush you, but I'm always here for you."

"I don't know why I'm crying. It was just sex, right? It shouldn't have meant anything."

"That's the biggest lie you've ever told me, Olivia. He was more than a single night a month. More than sex. If he'd just been sex, you'd have mentioned him in passing at least once over the course of your relationship with him. The fact that you didn't tells me you needed and wanted to keep him close to your heart. I get that. I truly do. He was yours, and he meant more than sex. Not that there's not emotion and need in sex, I know that more than most, but that's not what you had with Derek. At least not all of it. You might have held back your names, but I don't think you held back much else—no matter how hard you tried."

"I was just coming to that realization myself."

"That's good. Now you know why you're hurting. You're mourning the loss of a relationship that was far different than the label you put on it, and in doing so, you're bringing back all those memories you've fought so hard to not only forget, but also work through. You're allowed to cry, you're allowed to rage. You're allowed to do what you need to do. You told me you didn't want to continue as you were with Derek without him knowing about your past. Now he knows. The thing is, I don't know what reaction I expected since I don't know him."

Alice sighed, and Olivia wiped the tears from her face and filled her friend in on everything she hadn't told her before.

"I think he reacted exactly how I thought he would. Exactly how the Derek I've grown to know would. I don't know if he blames me for what happened to Stacey and, honestly, I think he believed me when I told him I didn't know our other connection until that night last month, but the thing is, that's not everything. He could look at me and see Stacey every single instance, and that will color every interaction we have until the end of time. And I don't think we're going to get that time. The thing is, it hurts. I hate it. But it's not like I can force myself into the situation. I didn't do anything wrong." She paused, let out a breath as the realization settled over her. "I didn't do anything wrong, but that doesn't mean it's going to work out with Derek. There are so many complications, it's not even funny. He might have told me before I told him the truth that he wanted more, but that was without all the facts. And he's not calling me or at my door so…"

"He doesn't have your number, baby."

"He could have gotten it from Austin. And he knows where I live. The ball is literally in his court, and even though it's killing me, I don't think I'd blame him if he wants to stay away. It's a lot."

"Then know you're the Olivia you need to be. It sucks. I don't have better words, and I'm an author, so you would think I'd be the one to come through for you with that, but it just sucks. I'm so sorry, hon. I hope he comes out of his shock and finds you, but if he can't or if *you* can't, then just…just *be*. Love you, Liv."

Alice never called her Liv since the author tended to hate nicknames, but today was a weird day, and their phone call wasn't easy.

"Thanks, Alice. For everything. And love you, too."

"Always, baby girl."

Olivia hung up and let out a breath. The screen in front of her had turned dark since she hadn't used it for too long, and she tried not to think if that was some form of metaphor for her life. Her life wasn't dark, her end wasn't near. She'd keep moving, just a little more bruised and battered than she was before.

The knock on the door pulled her from her thoughts, and she almost dropped her phone and her computer from her lap. She didn't know who could be at her door since she wasn't expecting a delivery, but there were always times when she forgot she had ordered something online.

She was only wearing old leggings with a tank and a sports bra since she had the hilarious idea that she'd go jogging later to work off some stress. Maybe run from her own demons if possible. Sure, like that would ever happen with her oncoming headache. Hopefully, the delivery man wouldn't mind her outfit.

When she went to open the door, however, it wasn't a delivery man or the one person a tiny part of her had wanted it to be—the part that pulled at her stomach and made her ache.

"Sierra. Is everything okay with the kids? Austin?"

Sierra Montgomery stood on her doorstep, looking wonderfully put-together as always and holding a plate of what looked like cheesecake brownies.

"Hey there. Can I come in? I won't take long, but I have sugar and hugs, and I think you could use both."

Of course, Sierra would know. Derek and Austin were friends, close friends, apparently, and Austin would tell Sierra if he knew.

So Olivia took a step back and braced herself for what was to come.

"I'm glad the boys are okay then," Olivia said woodenly, her eyes on the brownies and not Sierra. She hadn't eaten all day, and she was suddenly ravenous.

"They're great. Leif is getting all deep-voiced with the cracking, and it's adorable and scary. Colin is all smiles and laughter, and I never want that to stop. Austin? Well, Austin is part of the reason I'm here. Can I sit? The brownies are for you."

"Oh! I'm sorry, take a seat." They both sat on the couch, and each took a brownie. Olivia did her best not to make moaning sounds, but it was difficult.

"I'm going to tell you that these are not my brownies. Hailey from Taboo, the café next to the tattoo shop, made them and gave them to me for you."

Olivia's eyes popped up. "She knows me?"

Sierra shook her head. "No, but, apparently, Derek looked like he'd been kicked in the gut today at work, and Hailey gave half of the brownies to Derek to cheer him up, then Austin asked for the rest for you. Austin told Hailey and then me that the only reason Derek would look the way he did today was because of you, and that meant you deserved them, too." Sierra winced. "I don't know what happened, hon, and I'm sorry that I've been so busy I haven't been around to find out more. Yes, Austin and Derek are friends, but I don't want you to think that you're alone. Derek has been tight-lipped over the years, so I don't know him as well as I do some of the other artists. The fact that you and he seem to know each other shocked me as much as it did Austin."

"Small world and all that." Olivia played with the edge of her brownie, no longer hungry.

"Too small sometimes, and I get that. Before I married into the Montgomerys, I held everything back and tried not to let the world in. I was safer that way. I'm not saying that was wrong either, but I'm glad I changed the way I did when I met the Montgomerys. Derek isn't a Montgomery. He's always seemed open about who he is, but he's also been good about keeping parts of himself hidden. I get that. It's his business, and we Montgomerys can't make everyone spill their secrets."

Olivia snorted at that. "You're pretty good at trying, though."

Sierra just smiled. "True. I'm going to leave the brownies with you, and I won't pry. Just know that Derek looks like...well, Austin said he looked like he was hurting, and now that I'm looking at you, I'm going to tell you that you look the same. I don't know what happened, and I don't know if I can help, but I'm here if you need me. I'll leave you be with the chocolate, and when and if you're ready, know I'm right next door."

And with that, the other woman hugged her tightly and walked out the front door without another word, leaving Olivia standing there, wondering what the hell had happened.

The Montgomerys might not know what was going on between Olivia and Derek, but they were still trying to help, and that meant more than she could say. But she didn't know what she thought about everything else.

Derek was hurting? Of course he was, she'd known as much by the way he looked in the hotel room.

But what could she do about it?

She'd told the truth, and they'd both ended up hurt.

Now, she just had to find a way to move on.

Without him.

Someone knocked on the door again, and Olivia assumed Sierra must have forgotten something. She did a quick look around to see if the other woman had dropped something, but she didn't see anything. Maybe she had a few more words for Olivia and, honestly, she didn't mind since she liked the other woman.

"Did you forget something?" Olivia asked as she opened the door and froze, her palms going damp, and her hands shaking.

It wasn't Sierra.

No, it wasn't Sierra at all.

"Derek," she croaked. This couldn't be real. He couldn't be on her doorstep when she was trying to get over what they could have had. She was going to be just fine without him, but he couldn't be near her if that was going to happen.

But he was here.

Why was he here?

She couldn't hope. She couldn't dream. And right then, she couldn't even breathe.

"Olivia." He cleared his throat. "Can I come in? I think we should talk."

Without words, she took a step back and let him in. The door closed behind them both, and she turned to him, holding her hands close to her stomach.

Then she blinked.

Because Derek was in her house. Her home.

And she had no idea what might happen next.

Chapter Ten

Derek had no idea what he was going to say. He'd come up with ideas and then, as soon as he saw Olivia and the wide-eyed look of a woman deeply hurt by his actions, all of those ideas had slipped right from his mind.

She stood in front of him wearing soft leggings and a shirt that had seen better days, with her hair piled on the top of her head in a clip thing. And she'd never looked sexier. Even with the redness of her eyes and the puffiness of her face that told him she'd been crying, he thought her beautiful.

And he'd been the one to put those tears in her eyes and that look on her face.

Him.

Because he hadn't been able to stay when he should have. Because he'd been blindsided and needed time to think. It might have been what he needed, but he'd hurt her in the process, and now he'd just have to hope that she would forgive him for it.

"Thanks for letting me in," he said, not sure where to start. He was better with his hands and his words when it came to others. He was never one to easily figure out what to do with his own life and decisions, but he could help others work through theirs.

Now, he needed to work for himself.

And hope to hell that Olivia understood.

"I'm honestly surprised you're here." She wrung her hands in front of her, then let out a little half laugh, half sigh. "And I have no idea what to say to you. Should I ask you to sit down? Offer tea? A beer? I'm not the best at social interactions on a good day, but with you? I'm so far out of my depth, it's not even funny."

Derek reached out to take her hand, thought better of it, then did it anyway. Her eyes widened, but she didn't pull away.

"I don't need to sit. I don't need a drink. And I hate the fact that we're so awkward around each other right now. The one thing we never were before was awkward." He paused. "Even when we were kids."

"Derek. You don't have to talk about that…that time."

"I know, but the thing is, I think I do need to talk about it. I don't have anyone to talk about it with now."

"What do you mean?" she asked, a frown on her face.

Derek let out a breath. He hadn't meant to get into this part, but he needed her to know everything. There could be no more secrets between the two of them.

"Maybe we should sit down," he said softly. "It's a long story."

"They always are," she said wryly before taking her hand back and leading him to the living room. He'd seen her place before and had wanted to see more, wanted to know more about her, and he hoped that after they talked today, she'd let him into her life beyond noticing the color of the couch and throw pillows.

They'd just have to see.

Soon, they were sitting next to each other, the awkwardness settling in, so he just started talking. The quicker he got this part over with, the faster they could get to the part he'd actually tried to practice.

"After the accident, my mom pulled me out of school, pulled me out of everything really. She wanted to keep me safe all while not really talking to me. Dad let it happen because he…well, he didn't care."

"Derek."

"No, it's the truth. Mom went into an overprotective and blaming mode. Dad went into a weird ice mode where he pulled away from everything and everyone. We moved soon after the accident, Mom not wanting to be near where Stacey had been." He paused. "I never saw you again after the funeral. And even then, I don't remember much about that. You know?"

She reached out and gripped his hand, and he held onto her, grateful that she'd been the one to touch him this time.

"I don't remember the funeral at all," Olivia said. "I thought I might one day, but I think my mind blocked it. It didn't block the day everything happened, but it did block that."

"We were both kids, Olivia. Of course, our minds wouldn't let us remember everything." He cleared his throat. "Anyway, Dad didn't last in the house. He left us pretty quickly, and Mom broke down. I don't really think she ever put herself back together again, though I've tried to help with that. She's...she's not the same. Not well. And no matter how much help she gets, she'll always rely on me to keep her together even if she doesn't really want that."

"That's horrible, Derek. I'm so, so sorry."

"It *is* horrible, but it's not my whole life, Olivia. That's what I'm trying to circle around. What happened before when we were kids was a horrible accident. But it *was* an accident. I never once blamed you for what happened. I never even blamed the driver. I think I blamed God for a while, but now I don't have any blame, just a sense of loss."

Olivia wiped her eyes, and he leaned forward to brush his thumb along her cheek, helping her. He loved touching her, *needed* to touch her.

"I blamed myself for too long, but until it all came back with you, I hadn't blamed myself in years."

"We were *kids*, Olivia. You didn't do anything wrong. You were warning her, and even if you weren't, you were playing. Hell, I blamed myself, not you. Never you."

"You?" Her eyes were wide. "Why on earth would you blame yourself? You weren't even there."

"You're right. I wasn't. I didn't protect my little sister. And, yeah, it doesn't make sense, but that's how our brains work through grief, through blame and nonsense until we can breathe again. But it was over twenty years ago, Olivia. And no matter what happened, we're not those kids anymore. Yeah, the scars still cover us, but they're not the only things about us."

"I just hate the fact that you look at me and remember her. That's why it hurts so much."

He let out a curse under his breath. "I look at the sky and remember her. I *always* remember her. She was my little sister. I *should* remember her. You being in my life now doesn't change that. Yeah, it brought some sore aspects of that memory back to the surface, but sometimes that happens on its own without anything to trigger it. It's not you, Olivia."

"But you left. You heard the truth, and you left. I understood that, though. It was too much. We...we were living in our own world with our own promises. There were no true promises between us to keep things going."

Derek leaned forward even more, cupping her cheeks. "I left because it all came back, not because of what you did or said. Because you didn't do anything. We've been circling around each other, being the faded parts of ourselves rather than facing each other. I was shocked, yes, but not because of what happened when we were kids, but because we were connected more than I'd ever thought. I shouldn't have left, but I should have taken a step long before this. We were only together once a month because I thought it would be easy. I thought I could walk away and not have to feel again, but I was wrong."

"What are you saying, Derek?"

"Be with me. Take a chance on me. I went into that hotel room wanting to ask you to be with me, to see what we could be outside of a room where we keep rules and try not to fall in too deep. But even when I told you to call me Derek, I knew I wanted more. I need more, Olivia. And I hope you do too because I want you in my life. You've always been a part of it, but on the periphery. Now, I want you to be part of all of it. Can you do that? Can you look at me and not only see Stacey but what we could have, as well? Stacey will always be a part of us, it's inevitable. And that's okay. She *should* be part of us, but not the biggest part, not the only part. I want you in my life, Olivia. But I need to know what you want, too."

Olivia blinked a few times, then smiled. "You...you surprise me more every time I see you. I thought it would be too much to see me and think of her, but you're right, Stacey is a part of my life no matter what." She turned her head, kissed the palm of his hand. "I don't know if it'll work, Derek. We know each other, but then again, we don't. I'm not ready to promise forevers, but I want to promise todays. I want so much more. Just like you. And I've been so scared to want that, terrified to even dare mention it. If I voiced it, then it would be real, and I could feel the hurt when it didn't happen."

Derek only had to lean forward a few inches to brush his lips along hers. She took a quick intake of breath before she kissed him back.

"I've always been afraid of forevers, but I've always loved our nights. I want more of them, Olivia. I want days, too. I want it all. But you need to tell me what you want exactly. I need the words from you, not just my wants."

"I want you, Derek. I told myself I shouldn't, but I always did. Those nights we had together were what I looked forward to every month, and I was always afraid that one time you wouldn't be there. That was my worst fear."

"I was always there, Olivia. I'm always going to be there."

He kissed her again, and she moaned beneath him.

"It won't be easy," she whispered. "We don't have all the answers."

He thought about learning each other, the fact that they would have to see who they were as a couple rather than just a promise. He thought about how she would fit into his complicated life, and how he could fit into Olivia's.

"We'll make it work. We fought for what we've had so far, and we'll keep fighting. But, Olivia? The reward is going to be worth it. Don't you think?"

She licked her lips, and he leaned back so he could watch her face. "It's already worth it, and I'm not afraid to work." She paused. "I'm just afraid to lose you."

"You won't lose me."

"Then show me."

Her eyes darkened, and he let out a little growl. "I thought you'd never ask."

Then he kissed her again, this time a little harder, a little longer, before standing up. "Derek?"

He grinned and then reached down to pick her up. "I figured our first time as an us, rather than an idea, should be in your bed. What do you say? We've made the hotel ours, but let's try something new."

She pointed down the hallway. "Second door on the right. Make it fast, Derek, before I wake up and realize this is all a dream."

He kissed her as he walked, making sure to keep her safe and not fall along the way. "It's our dream then, only a waking one."

When they got to the bedroom, he carefully set her down on the bed, then kissed her some more. Their hands roamed over each other, their breaths coming in pants. When he stripped her out of her clothes, he laughed some as he tried to take off her sports bra.

"This thing is the bane of my existence. Not so much with the sexy lace, you know?" she said with a sultry laugh.

"You're so fucking sexy," he growled then bent over her so he could take one dark nipple into his mouth. Then he sucked on the other one, and she arched against him.

He quickly licked down her body before kissing her right over her wet and hot pussy. When she called his name, he leaned back and stripped out of his clothes, not wanting a single barrier between them except for the condom he slid along his length. He would discuss that and more with her later, but for now, it was just the two of them, the feel of them, their need.

"I'm going to taste more of you later, but I need to be inside you, Liv. I need more of you. Can you handle me? Make it just us, quick and hard, then go soft and slow next time?"

She licked her lips, then reached between their bodies, gripping the base of his cock tightly enough to make his eyes cross.

"I can do that. I know your body, Derek. You know mine. Let's remind each other of that, then learn the rest."

"I can do that." He leaned down and kissed her again, needing her taste, then slowly, oh so slowly, he entered her. Her heat, tight, wet, and perfect for him. As soon as he was fully seated, she lifted her hips, squeezing him even more, then gasped.

"Move, Derek. I need you to move."

"For you? Always."

And he *moved*.

They kissed, touched, and arched for each other until she came around him, and he followed soon after. He didn't stop touching her even as they lay together before going for another round, this one slower, and somehow, even hotter.

He had his Olivia, the woman of his dreams, the woman who had been the center of his nights and what he looked forward to each month for far too long, and he knew he'd want for nothing else.

She was his everything, and he couldn't wait to learn more of her in the coming days, over the coming nights.

Because she was truly his, just as he was hers.

And despite the rules he'd given himself, he'd learned her and would learn more. He'd have more than a single night a month, and he'd make all the promises in the world.

And in the end, he'd keep them.

For her.

His Olivia.

His promise.

His future.

His.

Epilogue

Olivia brushed her hair back from her shoulders, missing the long length, but enjoying her new inverted bob. It took less time to deal with in the mornings, and with everything going on in her life, she needed that time.

With a smile, she took a sip of her martini and looked around the hotel bar. There were a few businessmen around, mostly keeping to themselves, but there were a few giving her looks, as well. She ignored them since she wasn't here for them.

No, she was here for *him*.

And herself, of course.

It wasn't just for *him* that she'd put on a slinky wine-colored dress and heels that would hurt her back later, but thankfully, she wouldn't be keeping them on long. Of course, if *he* didn't get here soon, she might just have to slip them off her feet soon, but she wasn't going to do that quite yet.

There was still time.

"Is this seat taken?"

Again, that deep rumble of a voice sent shivers down her body, and she crossed her legs to keep her lady parts in check. They seemed to have a mind of their own when it came to a certain man and his voice.

She couldn't blame them, however.

She turned to see a very sexy man with longish hair and a beard she knew he kept clean and conditioned with a special beard care routine. In fact, he'd used the kit he received for Christmas on it that morning so it would smell of sandalwood and be soft against the inner silk of her thighs.

The man always took care of her by taking care of himself.

"You're welcome to sit," she said with a smile, "but I won't be here for long. I need to go upstairs."

His whiskey-colored eyes darkened. "Let me walk you then," he said, low, his voice so husky she squeezed her thighs together.

"Thank you."

She ignored the looks any others might be giving them and put her hand on his outstretched arm before going with him to the elevators. They were the only ones in their cab, but she didn't move closer, didn't brush her body against his even though she desperately wanted to. When they made it to the room at the end of the hallway, he took a key out of his pocket and pressed it against the sensor.

Then they were inside. The door closed behind them, and only the sound of her deep, ragged breaths filled her ears.

"You're so fucking sexy," Derek growled.

"You fill out those pants just fine," she said with a wink. "Is that your cellphone in your pocket, or are you happy to see me?"

He grinned, then winced when the cellphone in his pocket buzzed. "Shit, I need to take that. And, yeah, my cock is also hard for you, but still."

She just shook her head and went to sit on the bed, waiting for him to take the call. It wasn't his mother's ring, and even then she wouldn't have minded if it was his mom. She had been doing better over the years, but still needed to talk to her son every once in a while. Olivia knew the need and understood it, even if her relationship with the other woman wasn't exactly warm. It wasn't strained either, though, and Olivia counted that as a win.

"Yeah, she can have the purple drink. It's sugar-free, but she doesn't know that. And it's okay you called, that wasn't on the list, and if she's insistent, it's always better to call. Yeah, thanks. See you tonight." He hung up, and Olivia rolled her eyes.

"Stacey wanted the purple drink?" Their daughter was sweet and quiet and did her best to mind her manners, but she was in the middle of a purple phase, and that meant she wanted to eat and drink everything purple. The babysitter hadn't known that since it was a new thing, so the phone call made sense.

"She wouldn't drink anything else, and Kendra was worried." He set his phone on the table next to where she'd put her purse. "I was going to say, 'where were we,' but did that just kill the mood?"

She shook her head, her hair flowing around her face. "We're parents, husband of mine, we'll make do. Now, why don't you come to bed and show me exactly what's in those pants of yours?"

He chuckled and leaned over her, kissing her softly. "Since you asked so nicely."

Then he showed her, twice, and she fell in love with her husband, the love of her life, all over again. They didn't always get to play strangers like they were tonight, but every once in a while, their date nights were versions of what they had been before, and she loved it. She loved this man and all his facets and layers. He was her everything, and she knew that she was so damn blessed to have him in her life.

He was hers. Her Derek, her husband, her everything. He'd given her a baby girl who made her life even brighter. Olivia had inked butterflies down her back and sides that he kissed nightly. He knew her inside and out, and she knew that she'd cherish this time with him always.

Once, they'd only had nights. Now, they had forever.

She'd broken her rules, and she would always be grateful that she had.

She'd fallen in love.

She'd made her commitment.

And she'd told him everything.

Because he *was* her everything.

And now, as he held her close, she knew those nights had only been the beginning. Their inked nights to come would bring more heat, more love, and more of *them*.

For this night of the month, and every one to come. Finally.

* * * *

Also from 1001 Dark Nights and Carrie Ann Ryan, discover Wicked Wolf, Hidden Ink, and Adoring Ink.

Sign up for the 1001 Dark Nights Newsletter
and be entered to win a Tiffany Key necklace.

There's a contest every month!

Go to www.1001DarkNights.com to subscribe.

As a bonus, all subscribers will receive a free copy of
Discovery Bundle Three
Featuring stories by
Sidney Bristol, Darcy Burke, T. Gephart
Stacey Kennedy, Adriana Locke
JB Salsbury, and Erika Wilde

Discover 1001 Dark Nights Collection Five

Go to www.1001DarkNights.com for more information

BLAZE ERUPTING by Rebecca Zanetti
Scorpius Syndrome/A Brigade Novella

ROUGH RIDE by Kristen Ashley
A Chaos Novella

HAWKYN by Larissa Ione
A Demonica Underworld Novella

RIDE DIRTY by Laura Kaye
A Raven Riders Novella

ROME'S CHANCE by Joanna Wylde
A Reapers MC Novella

THE MARRIAGE ARRANGEMENT by Jennifer Probst
A Marriage to a Billionaire Novella

SURRENDER by Elisabeth Naughton
A House of Sin Novella

INKED NIGHT by Carrie Ann Ryan
A Montgomery Ink Novella

ENVY by Rachel Van Dyken
An Eagle Elite Novella

PROTECTED by Lexi Blake
A Masters and Mercenaries Novella

THE PRINCE by Jennifer L. Armentrout
A Wicked Novella

PLEASE ME by J. Kenner
A Stark Ever After Novella

WOUND TIGHT by Lorelei James
A Rough Riders/Blacktop Cowboys Novella®

STRONG by Kylie Scott
A Stage Dive Novella

DRAGON NIGHT by Donna Grant
A Dark Kings Novella

TEMPTING BROOKE by Kristen Proby
A Big Sky Novella

HAUNTED BE THE HOLIDAYS by Heather Graham
A Krewe of Hunters Novella

CONTROL by K. Bromberg
An Everyday Heroes Novella

HUNKY HEARTBREAKER by Kendall Ryan
A Whiskey Kisses Novella

THE DARKEST CAPTIVE by Gena Showalter
A Lords of the Underworld Novella

Discover 1001 Dark Nights Collection One

Go to www.1001DarkNights.com for more information

FOREVER WICKED by Shayla Black
CRIMSON TWILIGHT by Heather Graham
CAPTURED IN SURRENDER by Liliana Hart
SILENT BITE: A SCANGUARDS WEDDING by Tina Folsom
DUNGEON GAMES by Lexi Blake
AZAGOTH by Larissa Ione
NEED YOU NOW by Lisa Renee Jones
SHOW ME, BABY by Cherise Sinclair
ROPED IN by Lorelei James
TEMPTED BY MIDNIGHT by Lara Adrian
THE FLAME by Christopher Rice
CARESS OF DARKNESS by Julie Kenner

Also from 1001 Dark Nights

TAME ME by J. Kenner

Discover 1001 Dark Nights Collection Two

Go to www.1001DarkNights.com for more information

WICKED WOLF by Carrie Ann Ryan
WHEN IRISH EYES ARE HAUNTING by Heather Graham
EASY WITH YOU by Kristen Proby
MASTER OF FREEDOM by Cherise Sinclair
CARESS OF PLEASURE by Julie Kenner
ADORED by Lexi Blake
HADES by Larissa Ione
RAVAGED by Elisabeth Naughton
DREAM OF YOU by Jennifer L. Armentrout
STRIPPED DOWN by Lorelei James
RAGE/KILLIAN by Alexandra Ivy/Laura Wright
DRAGON KING by Donna Grant
PURE WICKED by Shayla Black
HARD AS STEEL by Laura Kaye
STROKE OF MIDNIGHT by Lara Adrian
ALL HALLOWS EVE by Heather Graham
KISS THE FLAME by Christopher Rice
DARING HER LOVE by Melissa Foster
TEASED by Rebecca Zanetti
THE PROMISE OF SURRENDER by Liliana Hart

Also from 1001 Dark Nights

THE SURRENDER GATE By Christopher Rice
SERVICING THE TARGET By Cherise Sinclair

Discover 1001 Dark Nights Collection Three

Go to www.1001DarkNights.com for more information

HIDDEN INK by Carrie Ann Ryan
BLOOD ON THE BAYOU by Heather Graham
SEARCHING FOR MINE by Jennifer Probst
DANCE OF DESIRE by Christopher Rice
ROUGH RHYTHM by Tessa Bailey
DEVOTED by Lexi Blake
Z by Larissa Ione
FALLING UNDER YOU by Laurelin Paige
EASY FOR KEEPS by Kristen Proby
UNCHAINED by Elisabeth Naughton
HARD TO SERVE by Laura Kaye
DRAGON FEVER by Donna Grant
KAYDEN/SIMON by Alexandra Ivy/Laura Wright
STRUNG UP by Lorelei James
MIDNIGHT UNTAMED by Lara Adrian
TRICKED by Rebecca Zanetti
DIRTY WICKED by Shayla Black
THE ONLY ONE by Lauren Blakely
SWEET SURRENDER by Liliana Hart

Discover 1001 Dark Nights Collection Four

Go to www.1001DarkNights.com for more information

About Carrie Ann Ryan

New York Times and *USA Today* Bestselling Author Carrie Ann Ryan never thought she'd be a writer. Not really. No, she loved math and science and even went on to graduate school in chemistry. Yes, she read as a kid and devoured teen fiction and Harry Potter, but it wasn't until someone handed her a romance book in her late teens that she realized that there was something out there just for her. When another author suggested she use the voices in her head for good and not evil, The Redwood Pack and all her other stories were born.

Carrie Ann is a bestselling author of over twenty novels and novellas and has so much more on her mind (and on her spreadsheets *grins*) that she isn't planning on giving up her dream anytime soon.

www.CarrieAnnRyan.com

Discover More Carrie Ann Ryan

Adoring Ink
A Montgomery Ink Novella
By Carrie Ann Ryan

Holly Rose fell in love with a Montgomery, but left him when he couldn't love her back. She might have been the one to break the ties and ensure her ex's happy ending, but now Holly's afraid she's missed out on more than a chance at forever. Though she's always been the dependable good girl, she's ready to take a leap of faith and embark on the journey of a lifetime.

Brody Deacon loves ink, women, fast cars, and living life like there's no tomorrow. The thing is, he doesn't know if he *has* a tomorrow at all. When he sees Holly, he's not only intrigued, he also hears the warnings of danger in his head. She's too sweet, too innocent, and way too special for him. But when Holly asks him to help her grab the bull by the horns, he can't help but go all in.

As they explore Holly's bucket list and their own desires, Brody will have to make sure he doesn't fall too hard and too fast. Sometimes, people think happily ever afters don't happen for everyone, and Brody will have to face his demons and tell Holly the truth of what it means to truly live life to the fullest…even when they're both running out of time.

* * * *

Wicked Wolf
A Redwood Pack Novella
By Carrie Ann Ryan

The war between the Redwood Pack and the Centrals is one of wolf legend. Gina Eaton lost both of her parents when a member of their Pack betrayed them. Adopted by the Alpha of the Pack as a child, Gina grew up within the royal family to become an enforcer and protector of her den. She's always known fate can be a tricky and deceitful entity, but when she finds the one man that could be her mate, she might throw caution to the wind and follow the path set out for her, rather than forging one of her own.

Quinn Weston's mate walked out on him five years ago, severing their bond in the most brutal fashion. She not only left him a shattered shadow of himself, but their newborn son as well. Now, as the lieutenant of the Talon Pack's Alpha, he puts his whole being into two things: the safety of his Pack and his son.

When the two Alphas put Gina and Quinn together to find a way to ensure their treaties remain strong, fate has a plan of its own. Neither knows what will come of the Pack's alliance, let alone one between the two of them. The past paved their paths in blood and heartache, but it will take the strength of a promise and iron will to find their future.

* * * *

Hidden Ink
A Montgomery Ink Novella
By Carrie Ann Ryan

The Montgomery Ink series continues with the long-awaited romance between the café owner next door and the tattoo artist who's loved her from afar.

Hailey Monroe knows the world isn't always fair, but she's picked herself up from the ashes once before and if she needs to, she'll do it again. It's been years since she first spotted the tattoo artist with a scowl that made her heart skip a beat, but now she's finally gained the courage to approach him. Only it won't be about what their future could bring, but how to finish healing the scars from her past.

Sloane Gordon lived through the worst kinds of hell yet the

temptation next door sends him to another level. He's kept his distance because he knows what kind of man he is versus what kind of man Hailey needs. When she comes to him with a proposition that sends his mind whirling and his soul shattering, he'll do everything in his power to protect the woman he cares for and the secrets he's been forced to keep.

Adoring Ink
A Montgomery Ink Novella
By Carrie Ann Ryan
Now Available

Holly Rose fell in love with a Montgomery, but left him when he couldn't love her back. She might have been the one to break the ties and ensure her ex's happy ending, but now Holly's afraid she's missed out on more than a chance at forever. Though she's always been the dependable good girl, she's ready to take a leap of faith and embark on the journey of a lifetime.

Brody Deacon loves ink, women, fast cars, and living life like there's no tomorrow. The thing is, he doesn't know if he *has* a tomorrow at all. When he sees Holly, he's not only intrigued, he also hears the warnings of danger in his head. She's too sweet, too innocent, and way too special for him. But when Holly asks him to help her grab the bull by the horns, he can't help but go all in.

As they explore Holly's bucket list and their own desires, Brody will have to make sure he doesn't fall too hard and too fast. Sometimes, people think happily ever afters don't happen for everyone, and Brody will have to face his demons and tell Holly the truth of what it means to truly live life to the fullest…even when they're both running out of time.

* * * *

"You look good."

It had come out as a growl, and her eyes widened.

"Uh, thanks. You look good, too." She smiled softly, and he relaxed marginally even as his cock hardened. Yep, this might be a mistake, but it could be a mistake worth making.

"So, I thought we could go on a ride around the quarry so you can see the lights and experience how it feels to be on the back of the bike. Then we can grab something to eat if you want."

She licked her lips, and his gaze went straight to them. Shit. "That sounds good." She let out a breath. "I know this is crazy, but I just really wanted to do something different, you know? And I never just go out with random guys, especially ones I just met, but the others know you, so I felt, I don't know, safer."

He smiled then and held out his hand. "I'm not going to hurt you, Holly. I want to make sure you get to do the things you want but might be too scared to do." He knew all about being too scared, and he didn't want that kind of life for her.

She slid her smaller hand into his. "This is so weird, but I honestly can't wait."

He laughed and pulled her toward him on the porch. "I've been called weird before so that's okay."

She winced. "I meant the situation. Not you. I mean, you could be weird, and I just don't know it. That's not okay. And that's why I'm about to get on the back of a motorcycle with you even though I have no idea what I'm doing. Because today has been one crazy day."

"Tell me about it. Lock the door, and let's get to it. I have a feeling once you have the wind on your face and the feel of a bike beneath you, all those worries are going to go away." At least, that's how it worked for him.

"I hope so."

As soon as she'd locked the door, he headed them both toward the Harley. "Let me help you with your helmet." She nodded as he made sure it fit correctly and the straps were tightened under her chin. "Feel good?" Another nod, and he handed her a pair of special night glasses that would help with the glare and protect her eyes from the wind. "Now I'm going to get on, and you're going to put a hand on my shoulder and swing your leg over so you straddle the bike behind me."

She did as he asked, and he had to hold back a groan at the feeling of her warm body pressed against his. This ride just might kill him.

"Now, wrap your arms around my waist."

She did so and laughed. "Well, if this isn't a way to get girls to hold you close, I don't know what is."

He winked over his shoulder and patted her hands. "You know it, babe. I really just wanted you pressed against me."

She rolled her eyes, and he laughed. "Whatever, Brody."

He explained where they were going again as well as a few other things she needed to know.

"Hold tight," he said with a grin, but he was serious. She squeezed him, and he held back another groan. Yep, this woman was going to kill him, and he just might like it. He started the bike, and she let out a little gasp but didn't sound alarmed.

"Ready?" he called out.

She patted his back before locking her hands again. "Ready!"

Then they were off.

Until the end of his days, he would never forget the sounds of pure glee and wonder she made as he drove her through the residential roads. She squeezed him tightly when he went faster before becoming more comfortable. The night was absolutely perfect for this kind of ride as well because she would be able to see the stars when she looked up as soon as they got away from the main city lights.

They'd driven for almost an hour before he pulled off at the top of a large hill next to the foothills of the Rockies. This would be a perfect view for her, and it would give her some time to stretch since she wasn't used to riding like that.

"So, what do you think?" he asked as he helped her off.

She rubbed her butt and laughed. "I'm going to be sore, but it's the best kind of sore."

His mind once again went to dirty places, and from the blush on her cheeks, so did hers.

"Did you have fun?"

She nodded and looked out into the wilderness, her gaze enraptured. "Yes. I mean, just wow. I've known people with bikes, even dated a guy with one, but we never went out on it because of snow and work and every other excuse I could come up with."

She was probably talking about Jake, and for some reason, that annoyed him. He wasn't prone to jealousy, but right now, he didn't want her to be thinking of her ex.

"Would you want to do this again?" he asked, his voice a growl.

She looked over at him and nodded. "Riding a motorcycle? Yes. Riding with you?" A pause. "Yes. I mean, if you want to."

Knowing he might be doing something stupid, he turned to her and cupped her face. She licked her lips once again, and it took everything within him not to kiss her right then. "Any time you want to ride, just ask." Something else came to him, and he blurted the next part without thinking. "And, Holly? I want to show you more. Not just riding with me. But all the adventures you said you wanted to do. You'll have to explain them to me a bit, but I want to show you things. Have fun, and just do stuff you haven't ever done. Will you let me be part of this with you? Will you let me show you that adventure?"

"Why are you doing this?" she breathed.

"I don't know exactly," he answered honestly. "But I want to. Is that enough? At least, for now?"

"I think...I think this might be exactly what I need."

On behalf of 1001 Dark Nights,

Liz Berry and M.J. Rose would like to thank ~

Steve Berry
Doug Scofield
Kim Guidroz
Jillian Stein
InkSlinger PR
Dan Slater
Asha Hossain
Chris Graham
Fedora Chen
Kasi Alexander
Jessica Johns
Dylan Stockton
Richard Blake
and Simon Lipskar

Made in the USA
Middletown, DE
21 June 2018